1ST SHOCK

SCHOCK SISTERS MYSTERY, BOOK 1

ADRIENNE GIORDANO
MISTY EVANS

1st Shock, A Schock Sisters Mystery, Book 1

Copyright © 2019 Misty Evans & Adrienne Giordano

Publisher: ALG Publishing, LLC

ISBN: 978-1-942504-33-7

Print ISBN: 978-1-942504-34-4

Cover Art by Fanderclai Design

Formatting by Beach Path Publishing, LLC

Editing by Gina Bernal, Elizabeth Neal

ACKNOWLEDGMENTS

Special thanks to John Leach who never seems to get tired of humoring Adrienne with answers to her wacky questions.

Huge gratitude and hugs to the Justice Team fans for following the Schock Sisters over to their very own series! If you haven't read the Justice Team and would like to, you can find their links in the back of the book.

As always, much appreciation to our families, friends, editors, and street teams for their amazing support!

1

MEG

My name is Megan Eleanor Schock and I rebuild the dead.

I'm not being dramatic either. As we speak, I'm contemplating Emily, a woman who sits in the corner of my office where I greet her every morning and promise justice. She's young. Probably a teenager, tossed away like trash and left to the utter warfare imposed on a human body when animals and Mother Nature feast on it.

I'm not even sure Emily is her name. All I know is when they come to me, usually via a law enforcement official trying to solve a cold case, I need to give them life. An identity someone stole from them.

My sister, Charlie, thinks I'm obsessed.

I damn well might be.

Ask if I care.

We formed a private investigation firm and share equal partnership in it. Charlie, a forensic psychologist and one hell of a profiler, does most of the investigating while I do the sculpting. Forensic sculpting is one of my specialties and I, unfortunately, have a steady stream of subjects to further hone my skills on.

One of those is Joseph—at least, that's the name I've given him. He was brought to me by a sheriff from Louisiana. It's yet another cold case that needs to be solved so I've volunteered my services to see if we can get this man identified. Maybe find his killer.

I peel my gaze from Emily and focus on Joseph. The chime of the back door sounds. Only staff and a certain other few come through it so this must be Matt, an investigator we hired to help with our caseload. Our only other employee is Haley, the receptionist, and I can hear her fielding calls at her desk near the front.

A second later, JJ Carrington, steps into my doorway. As usual, he's dressed to kill in an expensive gray suit, a crisp white shirt, and blue print tie. His dark hair is neatly combed and the artist in me itches to sketch him, to capture the perfect lines of his cheekbones and jaw.

At least until my eye snaps to the plastic shopping bag he's holding. "Swear to God, JJ, if that's what I think it is, I'll stab you."

Unruffled by my threat—he's dealt with far worse than me —the US Attorney for the District of Columbia, aka the Emperor of Cold Cases, steps to the worktable beside Joseph and clears a small space amongst my sculpting tools. He gingerly sets it down and I know, without a doubt, he's brought me yet another victim.

In a goddamned shopping bag.

For that alone I should maim him. Who am I kidding? JJ only brings me the ones investigators are absolutely stumped on.

Or that are possibly related to another case.

A case like the one from when I was in sixth grade and nine —I remember the number quite clearly—other sixth graders in the area went missing. My mother cried every time a child vanished and I spent the whole of my sixth grade paranoid I'd disappear too. That turmoil still sticks. No matter how old I get, it sticks.

To this day, none of those children have been discovered.

Not one.

I guess I keep hoping someday one of their skulls will come my way, and I'll be able to help give them justice.

That case has made me a freak about my loved ones and the idea of a family having to live with the heartbreak of a missing person. Add to that my artistic talent and watching my older sister immerse herself into the justice system and here I am. Ready, willing and completely able to help. I can't say it's fun, but it satisfies something in me. Makes me feel as if I'm doing my part in some small way.

JJ points to the bag. "Found eighteen months ago in Rock Creek park. Zero leads. If we don't come up with something, the case will go unsolved. There's some public safety group making noise about the area being unsafe."

"Crimes happen in plenty of parks."

"Tell me about it. We're getting pressure from the National Park Service who doesn't want this case used for propaganda."

I peek inside and see a cast of a human skull. When it comes to my work, I'm only ever brought duplicates made from molds taken of the actual victims.

"And you put him in a shopping bag?"

"I didn't say it's a him."

I like JJ, but his years as a prosecutor have gobbled up the last of his sensitivity. "Well, I'm not calling him—or her—*it* so until I determine a gender, he's a him."

I peel back the sides and, using both hands lift him, studying the eye sockets and teeth. It's small and I immediately question myself. A woman then, perhaps. Just like Emily, who has sat in my office, each day reminding me her killer is still out there. Her case has suffered dead end after dead end, each lead fizzling and leaving investigators at a loss. For that reason, I can't let her go. Or give up on her. Maybe because she's young and pretty and deserved an ending far better than the one she got. All I know is I'm determined to help her.

"Small head," I comment.

"A child?"

"I didn't say that. Maybe a woman. We'll see."

I set Avery—a nice, gender neutral name—back on the table and walk to the narrow storage closet where I keep extra sculpting stands.

"Tell me about her," I say as I place the skull on one. "Do we have the rest of her?"

"Not all, but some. ME has them."

"Animals got to her?"

JJ shrugs. "I'm guessing. They searched the area around the body, but we're still missing twenty-five percent of the bones."

Like I said, the wrath of the elements. "Cause of death?"

"Based on fractures in the neck area, ME says asphyxiation."

Interesting. "Can I see what you have?"

I have a process and part of it is seeing all the bones, getting the measurements and figuring out the person's height and age.

JJ nods. Of course. He knows I'm good. The myriad of awards hanging in our reception area attest to it. Plus, this isn't his first rodeo.

I circle the stand, examining the back, running one hand over the smoothness. I reach the front, my fingers lightly touching Avery's cheek and lower jaw and something inside me fires.

"JJ."

At the sound of my sister's voice, I glance at the doorway where Charlie's gaze is glued to the Emperor. He smiles at her and the energy in the room changes. Charlie and JJ have a...thing. Insane chemistry that crackles between them every time they get within ten feet of each other. I'd like to tell them to get a room, but their relationship is complicated. He's in the process of a divorce and my sister doesn't screw married men. He's been separated over a year, but until he works out his marital issues, Charlie has deemed him untouchable.

Even so, I'm a little jealous. I haven't felt that kind of passion in a long time and I miss the buzz that comes with it. Unfortunately, I have too many victims parading in and out of my life to focus on any living, breathing man that might spark something.

Like I said, Charlie thinks I'm obsessed.

As the stare down between them continues, she leans against the doorjamb and crosses her legs. She's wearing one of those fitted pencil skirts she likes and a blouse straight out of Vogue. Me? I play with paints all day. I'm a ripped jeans and T-shirt girl.

Charlie appears relaxed, but inside she's seething. I sense it in her slightly puckered and expertly lipsticked mouth.

"If you've brought her that skull," Charlie says, "I'll kill you."

Poor JJ. First I threaten to stab him and now Charlie will kill him. Our threats come for two very different reasons. I'm pissed about the shopping bag.

Charlie the skull.

JJ holds up both hands. "We need help with this one."

"I'm sure." Charlie nudges her chin at me. "But look at her, she's already bonding."

"I'm fine," I say.

My sister rolls her eyes. She knows me. Understands the second I put my hands on someone, they become part of me.

I look back at Avery. "This is Avery. She'll be staying for a bit. JJ tell the ME I'd like to come by in the morning. After that, I need to finish Joseph." I point to the other skull. "Once I'm done with him, I'll work on Avery."

Charlie straightens and points at JJ. "You. In my office."

2

CHARLIE

J'm worried about my sister.

I'm pissed at the man in front of me.

Story of my life.

"What do you think you're doing?" I ask JJ as I lean on my desk, crossing my arms under my chest and giving him my best glare. I've practiced it for hours in the mirror, getting it just right to make men cower under it. Women too, if they get in my way.

JJ meets my stare with the crooked grin that irritates the crap out of me. His eyes start at my three-inch Louboutins and creep up my legs to my hips, the grin growing wider when he stops at my generous rack. I hold perfectly still, ignoring the way my pulse trips all over itself.

Breathe, dammit. Do not let him get to you.

Fat chance that.

Finally, his gaze moves to my lips then locks with mine. "What do you mean, Charlize?"

JJ Carrington III knows exactly what I mean. He's always pushing me, taunting me, teasing me. Just like using my full name. He tells me it's so much sexier than the gender confusing Charlie.

"Why did you come in the back door?"

His eyes spark, ready for a sparring match. "The two measly spots out front were taken."

I'm a forensic psychologist, a former FBI profiler. I'm loyal to a fault but I'm a born skeptic. I question everything, including everyone's motives. "Correction, you deliberately parked in the rear lot and came in that way so you could avoid my office, and this very discussion, before talking to Meg. You brought the skull in a *plastic shopping bag*."

He lifts his hands, palms up, supplicating. Pretending not to know what the big deal is. "Walking around in broad daylight with a human skull tends to freak people out."

"You knew she'd be incensed and immediately champion for the person it represents. Which would lead to her bonding with the damn skull and offering her services, because that's what she does. You know that and took advantage."

The US Attorney for the District of Columbia handles local and federal cases. He oozes confidence, power, and control.

I have a thing for powerful, sexy men...and this one? Off. The. Charts.

He takes a slow, deliberate step toward me, staying just out of my personal space. Teasing once again. "You and I both know there is no one on God's green earth that can manipulate either of the Schock sisters. If Meg didn't want to do it, she would have said no."

"When was the last time Meg said no to a cold case?"

"When was the last time you did?"

Damn him. I talk a good game, but I'm just as obsessed as Meg, and he knows it. One of the reasons I left the FBI was all the red tape. Things move too slowly with them, there were too many rules. I'm all for them, but swift resolution is equally important. Families deserve closure, victims retribution.

"The local PD doesn't have it in the budget to get a recon-struction done," JJ finally admits, then rattles some other excuse about a public service group and the National Park Service giving his office grief.

We are not getting paid. Again. I reach over and tap a stack of files on my desk. "These are all paying clients. They deserve to come first, and since I'm not only the lead investigator around here, but also the accountant, I can tell you we don't have it in ours either."

"Give the paying clients to Mad Dog. He can handle them."

The other reason I left the FBI was to take care of Meg. Then Matt came along, and it was like we expanded our family. He became our younger brother. I have a responsibility to them to keep Schock Sister Investigations successful. Profitable. To watch out for them and our receptionist, Haley.

JJ inches toward me, officially crossing the boundary of my personal space. My pulse, already wonky, goes Code Red. "I need you on this too, Charlize. I don't think reconstructing the skull will be enough." Another step. "I need someone familiar with cold cases, murder cases. Come on, say you'll do it."

"You think murder is involved?" Dumb question, of course he does. Most bodies don't end up buried in a park. "Never mind. The answer is still no."

My sister doesn't know about this—no one but JJ and I do —but we slept together last year at a crime and evidence conference in Milwaukee. I didn't even know he was going to be there. I'd been asked to sit on a panel and had been enjoying myself in the thick of what I do best. Worrying too much about Meg and Matt took a backseat.

Then, as I looked over the group attending our session, I saw a familiar six-foot-four, dark haired man in a flashy Brioni suit. He gave me a wolfish grin and asked a question—I forget now what it was—and later, I drank too much brandy and ended up seducing him.

It was the easiest seduction ever.

Yes, he'd been separated from his wife for nearly a year, but that was no excuse. I never should've done it. I've tried to wipe it from my mind.

But when he's this close? When I smell his aftershave that reminds me of the ocean and see the blue flecks in his gray eyes? I remember *every moment* of our night. The way he touched me, licked me, made me moan. The way we made love over and over again, as if we knew it was a one-time gig. We had to suck every ounce of pleasure from that weekend. And we did.

Worse? I want to do it again.

I lick my lips, having already forgotten JJ's question.

His gaze drops to my mouth. The grin appears. He's spontaneous and fun, like sex was in Milwaukee, and I wish I could be that way too.

But I'm not.

I promise myself no matter how my pulse is going wild and I desperately want a repeat of Milwaukee, I will not sleep with this man again until he's free.

"I brought you a present," JJ says, reaching into his inside breast pocket.

He pulls out an envelope. I open it to find a picture with a phone number. The woman staring back at me is of mixed heritage, her tawny skin decorated with freckles, her bright green eyes in contrast to her dark corkscrew curls.

"Who is she?" What I'm really thinking is, *how is this a gift?*

"Juanita Jones, works in my office. Adopted right after birth. She was recently diagnosed with stage four lymphoma and it's metastasized. She wants to find her birth parents before she dies, and it appears she's located the mother."

I'm a genealogist in my spare time. People hire me to find lost relatives or create family trees. Back in the day before the Internet, my dad loved to work on our family tree. When he

ADRIENNE GIORDANO & MISTY EVANS

was on leave from the Army, we often spent Saturday afternoons in the basement at the local library, going through their genealogy collection. Not a big library, but one of the best in the area for tracking down your ancestors. Dad's love of personal history inspired my own. I've taken what he started and expanded it to include multiple trees and thousands of records. Once in a while Dad and I still go to the library and spend the afternoon working on other people's.

"She found her mom, so what's the problem?" I ask.

"The birth mother is German and claims the father is Polish."

I glance at the photo, Juanita's skin and hair telling a different DNA story. "People lie all the time about these things. Or block out memories they don't want, like being raped or the fact they slept around and don't actually know who the father is. No name listed on the birth certificate, I take it?"

He shakes his head.

"What do you want me to do about it?"

"Juanita's willing to pay a lot to get this resolved. Time is an issue, of course. Thought you might be interested. She wants answers, whether you find them through that ancestry website you use, or you help her mom remember the truth."

JJ is good. He knows I love a mystery, and I'm as much of a sucker for helping people as my sister. "I'll give her a call and see what I can do."

He reaches out, touches my cheek. "Next time, I promise to come through the front and check in with you before I talk to Meg, okay?"

Who's being manipulated now? JJ knows how to negotiate, make concessions, and get what he wants. It's how he landed the job he has. If only he could get his wife to let him go.

He doesn't wait for my answer. I watch him leave my office and take a deep breath, forcing my pulse to slow.

I miss him already.

Tossing Juanita's picture on the desktop, I stare at it for a moment, wondering what secrets her mother is keeping, if I'll be able to get the answers she seeks.

"Who's that?" Meg is in my doorway, no doubt checking on me after JJ's departure. She points at the photo on my desk.

"Another person who needs our help."

The haunted look in my sister's eyes reflects my own.

"There are too many, Charlie."

This I know. It's what drives me to get out of bed every morning. "Matt can handle these." I tap the stack of folders. "I'll help with Avery, okay?"

She gives me a tiny smile before heading back to her office. I see the look in her eyes, the one that says we're not so different under the clothes and attitudes. We're both on a mission.

And maybe we're both a little obsessed with it.

3

MEG

I stand in the hallway next to the Medical Examiner's office waiting for Dr. Janelle Gentry, deputy chief of the Death Investigations unit, to usher me into her lair. The place where all the action happens.

I close my eyes for a second, grounding myself. Even in a morgue, I can do a quick meditation. A moment or two where I release any anxiety about murder victims and facing them day in and day out.

Soon, I'll be shown Avery's bones. Minus, of course, the twenty-five percent of her that's still scattered among the trees in Rock Creek Park. The idea of her flesh being torn apart by animals burns inside me, tears right through my stomach.

I want all of her. Every bit that can be given a proper burial once we discover who she is and why she left this earth.

Yes, I'm determined. And hopeful. It's morning and the day hasn't had a chance to wear me down.

Yet.

I like to do these meetings early for just that reason. My mind is sharper and I'm less emotional.

So many victims. So little time.

Breathe.

I inhale and focus on my mantra. On letting my thoughts go.

Time passes, I'm not sure how much. Maybe three minutes, could be ten. All I know is I'm coming out of my meditation. My mind is clear, my previously jittery nerves calm and I'm ready for the task ahead. Slowly, I open my eyes. I've learned if I come out of this too fast, my body will rebel. I'll feel...off...for the rest of the day. Fatigue, headache, tension. It'll all be there, dragging me down.

Another few minutes pass and I let out a final deep breath as the swish of a door sounds.

Dr. Gentry, a woman in her forties with rich auburn hair—probably not her natural color given the wisps of gray popping up—and a penchant for pantsuits stands in the doorway. "Good morning, Meg."

As usual, her smile is warm, lighting up her angular face. Like me, she still has hope for the day.

We've worked together on cases before, most notably Simon Worth, the twelve-year-old who'd gone missing in 1979. Eight months ago his remains were found buried under a building that'd been knocked down in preparation for a new strip mall. One of the workers stepped off the backhoe and—whoopsie—there's a skull. Talk about a crappy morning.

"Hi. Thank you for seeing me on such short notice."

She waves it off. "No problem at all. JJ is all over me on this one."

"He brought me the skull yesterday."

"Name?"

I smile. My habits are well-known amongst the ME's staff. "Avery."

We move through another set of doors and walk past a room with a silver metal plate that says, "Body Storage." I haven't seen the inside of that room, but I'm told it can hold around two hundred corpses. I don't want to think about that number of bodies stacked up, most more than likely in terrible shape from a tragic death.

We move into one of the autopsy rooms—surgical suites— as Dr. Gentry calls them. It's spotless with the sharp antiseptic scent of a recent scrubbing. Lining the wall to my right is a long sink holding various metal and plastic containers, all apparently cleaned and neatly placed upside down on a draining tray. In the center of the room is a shiny metal table holding the skeletal remains of who I have to assume is Avery.

I'll get you home.

"This," Dr. Gentry says, "is your Avery."

My guess is, before my visit, the bones were removed from a carefully labeled cardboard box that sits on the lab's top shelf with all the others of unidentified remains. That's what they do with them. Shove 'em on a shelf until the case is solved or their family claims them. I glance up and see more than a dozen.

Random people who could be anyone's mother, brother, sister.

Child.

I can't think about it. Can't.

I shake it off and focus on Avery. Starting at her head, I walk around, making sure to keep my hands at my sides and take my time analyzing the bones and reconstruction of them.

"Petite," I say.

"We're estimating around five-one. Caucasian female."

I was right. This gives me a small sense of satisfaction since I originally doubted my instincts and went with the gender neutral name.

"Age?"

"Late teens to early twenties. Her teeth are in good shape."

Meaning vital DNA can be garnered from them and later tested for any possible matches. Something tells me that'd be too easy.

I study the teeth, my artist's eye narrowing in on the perfectly even top row. "Straight."

"Yes. No cavities either. She could afford dental work."

I retrieve my phone from my back pocket and make a note of it. Why this detail stands out, I'm not sure, but something down deep compels me to record it.

"Clothing?"

"A tank top, sports bra, and running shorts. All Nike and still on her body. She also wore a fitness watch. We found it on her wrist, but with the elements, it's dead."

Avery wasn't found naked, so either rape wasn't the intent, or she fought him off. *Good for you.*

"So, I'm going to assume, based on the clothing, watch, and dental work, she had money. Or at least wasn't destitute or homeless."

Dr. Gentry shrugs. "It's not a stretch."

Charlie would have to deal with that angle, but it gives us a starting point. Right about now, she'd be schmoozing detectives to turn over their notes. Knowing my sister, she has all this information already. She's good.

Really good.

Together, we are, in fact, remarkable.

I move my gaze to Avery's head where I see no cracks or holes from a bludgeoning or gunshot. The cast JJ brought me didn't show any signs of trauma either, but seeing the actual skull confirms it for me.

"What else?" I ask. "JJ said something about neck fractures."

I meet her eye and she points to Avery's neck. "Yes. The left arm of the hyoid has a fracture. It's about an eighth of an inch from the tip."

I peek at the top of her neck at the u-shaped bone and see the crooked left side. "I see it. Are you thinking strangulation? Maybe a rope or something?"

I'm anxious, ready to know the particulars of Avery's death so we can find her killer.

"Hyoid fractures are more common in ligature and manual strangulation as opposed to hanging. We're going with manual." She wraps her thumb and forefinger around her own neck. "The force of the hand covers a wider area and causes direct stress on the hyoid."

The demonstration allows me to visualize Avery with someone's hand—or hands—squeezing her throat. Stealing her air and cutting off all that vital blood supply.

Breaking a bone.

My stomach burns again and the sensation shoots in all directions, searing the underside of my skin.

I refocus. My job here is not to get emotional. Charlie reminds me of this often. Still, there is part of me that rejects it. Always. I'm an artist. Tapping into my emotions makes me good at my job. And if I can't get pissed about a young woman being strangled and tossed away like garbage, well, what would it take?

I picture my sister in front of me, shaking her head. What would I do without her? I just...no. Can't go there. I breathe in. Breathe out. "All right. What else?"

"Nothing remarkable," Dr. Gentry says, as if this whole Godforsaken thing is mundane. In her world, maybe it is so I stay quiet while she continues. "The rest of her, aside from a surgical screw in her knee, is free of injury."

Knee surgery. On the table in front of me are the skeletal remains of a young woman, possibly late teens to early twenties, with good teeth, found dressed in what some might consider fairly expensive athletic clothes and a fitness watch.

"My thought is she's a runner. Maybe not wealthy, but not poor either. A college student or millennial, out for a run. She's targeted by someone, more than likely a man—or very strong woman—who had enough strength to break a bone in her neck."

"That about sums it up."

"Which means," I say, "we only have to narrow her down from the other seventy thousand white, college-aged females in the D.C. area."

No wonder JJ, the Emperor of Cold Cases, brought Avery to us.

4

*A*pproximately four thousand unidentified bodies are recovered each year in the United States. Of those, one-fourth remain so after a year. Today, when I check NamUs —the National Missing and Unidentified Missing Persons database—there are over twelve thousand cases. The numbers are staggering and it's only getting worse.

JJ has already entered the new UIP case into the federal system, populating NGI, the FBI's Next Generation Identification database, as well as UNT, the Texas University whose lab specializes in DNA analysis, along with a dozen more. Not surprisingly, no matches have been found. In my head, I hear Meg say, *"It's too new. Give it another twenty-four hours. Something will pop up."*

Wish I had her optimism.

I sent a DNA collection kit with Meg to give Dr. Gentry. At least those are free, thanks to funding from the National Institute of Justice. It's a big if, but *if* I can get the Center for Human Identification at UNT to bump this case to the forefront, they'll run an analysis and confirm cause of death, which could help us solve the case. Of course, they'll need a reason to put it ahead of all the others, but I have JJ in my back pocket. He didn't bring us that skull to see it end up in a closet somewhere. What I need is a good lead, evidence that makes this high-profile.

My first call of the morning goes to the detective in charge of the case. The victim is UI and we're assuming it was a homicide. It goes to voicemail and I leave a message, offering lunch in exchange for information. No doubt, he has plenty of open cases stacked on his desk, crimes, homicides, and a lovely assortment of crap, demanding his constant attention. I know Ritter loves food though since I've worked with him before. He isn't one to turn down a free meal.

I pull out a red folder and label it Case UIP281. Organization is important, especially in this office where there are too many open files, and multiple people working each one. I attach a sheet on the left side, and another, similar to a chain of custody for evidence, on the other. The latter tracks communication, rather than physical evidence, between all the parties and reminds me who is responsible for what as we proceed.

I already have five players: JJ, Meg, Detective Ritter, Dr. Gentry, and myself. From the outer office comes the sound of the fax machine spitting something out. Methodically, I work through our standard intake form for new clients, inserting JJ as the contact person, and UNKNOWN for the name of our vic. I know more about the US attorney than the girl; her demographic data—age, height, weight, etc., remains a solid wall of blanks.

Matt breezes in my door, carrying a large white coffee cup from my favorite shop and a paper from the fax machine. He's dressed in jeans and a T-shirt with a casual dark blue jacket. His hair is a couple weeks past needing a trim and light brown bangs fall across his forehead. He sets the cup on my desk and drops into the chair, ready for our meeting. "Three shots of espresso, one cream, just the way you like it."

I thank him and peel off the lid, scanning the fax. Detective Ritter has sent me a hand-written detail sheet, probably because I dropped JJ's name in my voicemail, or maybe his wife has him on a new diet. Unfortunately, the details are circumstantial and slim. Late teens/early twenties, clothing intact, neck fracture. A watch was found with the victim. If it was a robbery gone bad, why didn't they take that? I realize this will slide to the bottom of the detective's cases, if it hasn't already.

The smell of coffee is so good I close my eyes for a second and inhale deeply before blowing on the liquid and taking a sip. I tuck the paper into the folder. Once Meg returns and I find out what she discovered at the coroner's, I'll add those tidbits of info into the national database entry. "Did you buy the ring?"

Matt shoots me his trademark "Mad Dog" grin, his eyes peering from under the bangs. "I'm going to let her pick her own. Safer that way."

He keeps finding excuses not to propose to his girlfriend, Taylor. "Chicken."

The grin fades and he throws up his hands in exasperation. "I don't know what she'd like, and I don't want to get it wrong. She's...you know..."

The coffee makes me feel halfway alive. I sip more. "Picky?"

"Choosy," he amends. "This is, like, the biggest thing I've ever done, Charlie. Call me chicken all you want, but I have a good reason to be scared of this woman. She's even more of a hardass than you."

So he believes.

I understand where he's coming from. Taylor is an FBI agent, and a damn good one. Missing Persons is her jam, just like mine and Meg's. "Two carats minimum, square cut, platinum band. It's not that hard, Matt."

"Square? I was thinking pear-shaped. Or maybe round."

I wiggle the pink topaz on my left hand. It's not an engagement ring, and I really shouldn't wear it, but I was feeling a bit sappy this morning after a sleepless night, thanks to dreams about JJ. Just talking about proposals and marriage makes me squirm. I try not to glance at the square gemstone—the only thing JJ's ever given me—but my sappiness betrays me, and I find my gaze slipping to the ring. It's a promise things will work out for me, for us. Most days, I don't believe JJ will ever make good on it.

Dammit. I need more coffee.

I need to throw the ring away.

"Taylor wears a square diamond pendant necklace when she dresses up." I clear my throat, set down the coffee. "The diamond studs she never takes out of her ears are also square." Squares and cubes are solid, balanced. Often, people who've been through trauma are drawn to that type of geometry. It is a foundation, a structure, support. Something you can lean on, build a relationship on. "I've never seen her wear much else in jewelry, so you want to keep it clean, no extra diamonds on the band or anything froufrou. Keep it understated and classy. Let the diamond be big and do the talking."

He is pensive for a moment, then the grin appears once more. "How about you go with me to pick it out? I have to meet with the Hughes family at two, probably take an hour or so. We could go after that. You need a break from the office. Meg too. You should both come."

Matt is the closest thing I'll ever have to a little brother, and I'd love to help with this, but neither of us will be free this afternoon. I reach over and pick up the stack of folders. "After you meet with them, I need you to dig into these clients. I've worked on the preliminaries for all three cases, so the initial research is done."

His bangs jump as his eyebrows lift, a silent question as to why I'm suddenly doubling his caseload.

"Our favorite US attorney brought us a new UIP," I explain. "I have to help Meg."

His question multiplies, the bangs jumping again. "I thought you swore off Carrington."

Personally, yes. "It is not in the best interest of the firm for me to turn down a direct request from the Justice Department." Even though I damn well tried.

"I'm not worried about the firm. I'm worried about you, Charlie."

This is why I think of Matt as my kid brother. He has a protective streak as long and as wide as my dad. *I should call him tonight. Get him started tracking down Juanita Jones' father.* "Meg is the one you should worry about. JJ brought her a replica of a skull."

Matt sinks low in his chair, his gaze shifting skyward. "Shit. Has she named it?"

"*It* is a girl." Meg appears in the doorway, looking excited. The coroner's office offered a clue, I can see it on her face. "*Her* name is Avery."

Gentry clearly confirmed the sex of the victim. Matt and I exchange a look. He stands and grabs the new cases, waving at us as he leaves. I open the red folder and grab my favorite pen. "I started a file. The number is UIP281. What did you learn?"

My hand is poised to write the details Meg uncovered. "Avery is not a case number. She's a person."

Meg never gives up, whether it's identifying one of her girls in the basement, as she refers to them, or reminding me to be human and embrace empathy. But Meg likes to dive deep into emotions. If I did that, I'd never make it back up for air. The ghosts of the dead would haunt me night and day. I have to maintain some distance, a certain level of detachment. "Ritter's notes show a fractured neck. Did Gentry confirm cause of death?"

"They're going with strangulation. She's sending out the kit today. Avery had straight teeth and no cavities. She could afford dental work. Also, Dr. Gentry doesn't suspect rape."

I can see this makes Meg happy. I note the details, confirming the same assumption Detective Ritter listed in his notes—sexual assault was unlikely. So she wasn't killed during an act of rape, and most likely not in a robbery scenario.

Meg continues talking, pacing as well. Knowing my sister, she'll start with a sketch then move to the skull. She uses it as a guide while she sculpts. It keeps her focused. As if that were ever an issue.

She holds up a finger. "Emily was found twenty miles from Avery. Same basic facts. Decent clothes, gold earrings. No evidence of rape. My gut tells me there's a connection. We need to look for crossover. A pattern."

Emily. Avery. A trickle of fear worms its way around my stomach. Meg is bright, creative, talented, and so driven, but some days, I feel like I'm losing her to these dead girls.

Dead girls. I hide my internal shudder. The neck fracture, the lack of rape...it reminds me of my last case as an FBI agent —one that still gives me nightmares. Mickey was such a loser, but a damn clever one. Bastard's in prison now, but his reign of terror still haunts me.

I call up the NamUs log and fill in a few more blanks with our inconclusive evidence. It's not much, but it's more than we had a few minutes ago. "I'll work on cross-matching strangulation cases in the local area." We don't know if Emily was strangled—she's another ghost with no obvious COD, but it'll make Meg happy if I at least act like I'm looking for a connection. "Off topic, Matt needs help picking out a ring for Taylor. Wanted to know if you could go with him later today and offer your wise counsel."

This gets a smile out of her, but it's short-lived when Haley buzzes my phone. "You have a visitor. A Ms. Juanita Jones? She doesn't have an appointment." Haley's voice lowers a fraction. "She said Mr. Carrington sent her."

Oh boy. This gal doesn't mess around. Guess I wouldn't either in her position. "Send her back," I tell Haley. Meg heads for the door, more than ready to escape to her studio. Before she disappears, I lay on some guilt. "Matt needs help, Meg, no lie. He was going to buy her a pear-shaped diamond."

Her head snaps up and she shoots me a look. "Please, no. She would hate that."

"We need to take care of this, steer him in the right direction."

"I'll talk to him."

In the hall, I hear her soft voice greet our visitor, then Juanita steps into my office. One hand shoots out and I rise to shake it across the desk. Her bracelets jangle. "Thank you for seeing me. I should've made an appointment, but... JJ said you wouldn't mind."

While beautiful, her skin has a gray cast to it, the brackets around her mouth are deep with concern. She wears a brightly colored scarf around her head, the corkscrew curls in the picture JJ gave me long gone.

"Please have a seat." I motion her into the chair Matt vacated, making a mental note to castrate JJ later. "Can I get you something? Water? Tea?"

"A shot of vodka?" She laughs, letting me know she's kidding. Sort of.

"I have brandy stashed in the bottom drawer."

She waves me off with a strained smile. "I'm not usually this pushy, please understand, but if you can't help me in the next few days, I need to know so I can find someone who can."

Something has changed with her prognosis. I can see it in her eyes, hear it in her voice. How long does she have? A few weeks? Days?

What am I supposed to say—*you've caught me at a bad time?*

When could be worse than knowing you're standing at death's door? "Have you taken a DNA test?"

"Yes, with Family Ties, the local outfit in D.C.. I sent one in several weeks ago after I found my birth mother and she claimed my father isn't black. I thought it'd give me a starting point, to prove at least where mine originates from, but the results aren't in yet."

Picking up my phone, I dial my friend at FT. "I may be able to expedite it, hang on."

Within minutes, I have confirmation from Jeri that Juanita's test results will be in her inbox by the next morning. If there are any matches in their database, she'll get notification of those too. My hope is that a distant cousin on her father's side will show up and we'll have a strong starting point to track down the man who shares his genes with Juanita. If I can get a name, I can check public records—birth certificates, marriage licenses, obituaries. I take down her mother's name and number and promise to speak with her as I show Juanita out.

Hours later, I'm still thinking about how to pose my questions to the birth mom when my mind circles back to Mickey Wilson, dead girls, and what Meg said right before she left my office this morning. *A pattern.*

I love patterns almost as much as I do squares. Sitting at my computer, I start cross-matching local UIP cases that match the late teens/early twenties profile with possible strangulation and no signs of rape.

Dinner time whizzes by as I delve into result after result. Eventually, I jump from my chair and head to Meg's studio, ready to bear hug my sister at her brilliance.

5

MEG

*I*t's late.

Actually, not that late, but I've been going since six this morning and my fuzzy brain is letting me know just how lax I've been in taking care of myself today.

Five years ago, I had my first panic attack. It came on suddenly and I swore I was in cardiac arrest. After being diagnosed with anxiety, I knew I didn't want to live in fear of these debilitating attacks and through meditation and various other relaxation techniques have kept them at bay. It's been fourteen months since my last episode, and I refuse to give in now.

Along with my drawing pad, I set my pencil on my lap, trapping it under my hand while I close my eyes. I've pushed myself too far, allowed my emotions to drain my energy reserves. It happens spending time with dead women. Usually, I can push through but the synapses in my brain aren't firing.

I can't let it stop me though. Five minutes. That's all I need for a quiet, meditative state that'll recharge me. As tired as I am, as much as I should call it a day and go home to bed, something nags at me, urging me to begin my sketch of Avery.

Every case starts with a composite image of the victim. As

humans our heads are anatomically similar. Generally speaking, we all have the same bones and muscles. Our differences come in the sizes and forms of them.

And that's where my sketches come in. Some forensic artists specialize in composite imagery, others age progression or reconstruction. Me? I have a twofer. Mine are composite imagery *and* reconstruction.

The former gives me a blueprint before I sculpt. The process allows extra time to dig deep, to focus and form a connection with the victim, something I need if I'm going to help the authorities find the predators.

"Meg!"

So much for quiet. Meditative state officially shattered, I pop my eyes open, stare straight ahead at Avery's skull mounted on the stand in front of me. I'll be lucky if I don't get a headache in the next ten minutes.

I turn and find my sister charging into my office/studio. She spots me sitting with the pad and pencil in my lap and slams to a halt, which is something to behold considering the ridiculous high heels she's wearing. We could feed a family of four for a month on what Charlie spends on a pair of shoes.

But, she works hard and donates more—way more—than her money when it comes to the pursuit of justice. Personally, I think the shoes and clothes are my sister's coping mechanism. When surrounded by violent death, we all need something.

And she won't allow herself to have JJ, so fancy shoes it is.

"Sorry," she says.

Clearly she's aware she's interrupted my meditation, but something has her wired and I firmly believe she's not sorry at all.

She lifts the red folder in her hand. "I think I've got something."

This perks me up. "What?"

"Patterns. You mentioned them this morning, and I kept

thinking about an old case, when I was still with the Bureau, so I ran a cross-check using the same markers as Avery. I entered her age, hair color, cause of death, no sexual assault, and a two-year time frame into the system."

My sister's rushed tone prods my weary brain to fire. I stand, setting my pad and pencil on my work table so I can peek at Charlie's notes. I inhale the faded, sweet-yet-spicy scent of her saffron and myrrh based lotion and realize she's had just as long of a day. Together, we'll work through this.

As always.

"Tell me," I say. "Wait. Let's go to the conference room so we can lay it all out."

I'm a visual person. I need everything in front of me and if my sister has gotten a hit or two from the various alphabet soup law enforcement databases she uses, I want to see what she has, absorb it and form conclusions.

I follow her down the short hallway, her feet moving amazingly fast on those stilt heels until she bursts into the room, her excitement flying off her like fireworks on July 4th.

I can't help but feel the energy, but I've been in this game long enough to know I can't get ahead of myself. Too many disappointments have crushed my ability to open up to the chance of success. I remain cautiously optimistic.

Charlie smacks the folder down, flips it open and spreads four sheets of paper side by side. "These are all hits. Four unsolved murders. The first three are females, blonde, not raped."

A wispy flutter cruises along my arms and I quickly skim the information. By the time I get to page four, we're into the good stuff. Skeletal remains found near interstate 495, otherwise known as the Capital Beltway, a road that intersects with I-270, and loops around D.C. in an almost perfect circle.

Charlie taps the page I'm reading. "She's an unidentified female."

"Another cold case."

"Yes."

So many damned cold cases.

I move back to the first victim. Ainsley Sinclair, a sophomore in college studying engineering. Charlie has also printed a color photo of Ainsley and I study it for a few seconds. Her platinum blond hair against a tanned face gives her a sunny, California-girl appearance. I flick my gaze back to page one for her personal details. Nope. Born and raised in Maryland.

"They're all blondes," Charlie says. "Well, except for the unidentified victim. Hers had already decomposed so we don't know her coloring. But, she fits the pattern. Young, female and probable strangulation."

A niggling on the back of my neck alerts me that something, I'm not sure what, is about to happen. Maybe we'll discover a clue, or we'll find, no matter how excited Charlie is, that these cases have nothing to do with each other.

I go back to Ainsley, check the location where her body was recovered. River Road.

Hmmm.

My sister is quiet, but I can feel her gaze on me. She knows I'm thinking, *knows* to let me gather my thoughts and not to interrupt my flow.

Finally, I look at her and she understands this is permission to charge ahead in her Charlie way.

She waggles her fingers. "What are you thinking?"

We store a computer tablet in the credenza and as Charlie talks, I grab it. A few taps at the screen shows me an image of the roadways around D.C. so I carry it to the giant whiteboard hanging on the wall at the far end of the room. I set the tablet on the lip of the board that holds markers, then scoop one of them up and draw a large circle. To the left of that, I place an intersecting line and label it River Road.

"Meg?"

I snap the marker against the board. "Roll with me here. Ainsley was discovered on River Road. Read the locations where the others were found."

Behind me, I hear the rustle of paper that indicates my sister is about to humor me. "Daphne Meadows was in the trees along the GW Parkway. Near the Beltway."

I check the image on the tablet and zoom in, finding where the Beltway intersects with the GW then draw another line before I turn back to Charlie. "Next."

Charlie sets the report down, grabs another page with fingers that move too quickly and can't quite grab it. Too much adrenaline. She slows down and slides it to her. "Arlington Boulevard West. Mark it."

I don't know all the exits along the Beltway, but I've driven it enough to know general areas. Somewhere on the middle-right of my circle is where Arlington Boulevard intersects.

Charlie studies my rendition and nods in approval.

Still standing next to the table, she rests her hands against the surface and reads the next profile. "Our unidentified victim. Come on, come on," she says. "Where are you?"

Her voice is clipped, her energy contained. Like me, she's learned not to get too far ahead of herself in case we're wrong.

This time, we're not. I can feel it.

"Got it!" Charlie says. "Braddock Road."

She drops the report and charges toward me. "Right here." She jabs at the approximate location. "Exit 54A or B off the Belt-way, depending on if you want East or West."

I draw the fourth and final intersecting line then step back to view my work. Charlie does the same, the two of us side by side, staring at my makeshift drawing of the Capital Beltway.

"My God," Charlie says.

"Young females. Blonde. Strangled."

"Found on the ring of the Beltway." Charlie spins to face me. She's as pale as the whiteboard. "Serial killer."

6

CHARLIE

*M*y damn watch is dead again.

Impatiently, I tap the dial, the hand stopped at five thirty-five AM. Two hours ago, before I even put the bloody thing on. I didn't notice, and now that I'm at my desk, I'm annoyed at my own incompetence.

I go through watch batteries like I do cups of coffee— too many, too often. My body seems to absorb the tiny storage cell's energy, choking off time. Or maybe, it's simply the force of mind. Like a Jedi, I need time to slow down or stop it long enough for me to catch up.

There will be no catching up today. I spent several hours last night researching our serial killer and filling out paperwork to try and get files on all the cold cases in the past two years that fit the parameters of Emily and Avery. I couldn't have slept anyway, my stomach churning like white water rapids. There's someone I know who could be the killer. Someone I testified before a jury about and helped put in prison nearly four years ago. He was into young, college-age girls, and took out his dysfunction on several before he was caught.

Mickey Wilson's attorney tried to get him off, saying he was not mentally competent to stand trial and needed psychological help. Don't all killers need psychological help? I was the forensic psychologist the prosecution called on to evaluate Wilson, and not only did I find him competent to stand trial, I knew he'd killed more than the three women they were charging him with.

The pattern Meg and I discovered could be a coincidence. That's why I need to find the cold cases in the last two years that fit. The more the better in order to analyze and establish with certainty that we have a serial killer.

While I'm waiting—it could be days or weeks before those files start trickling in—I'm following the one lead I have, Mickey.

I'm heading to Hazelton Penitentiary in West Virginia, a high-security United States federal prison for male inmates. A long drive, but one I hope proves fruitful.

I haven't told Meg because she'll want to go with me, and that place will give her nightmares for months. I've only been one other time and it took weeks to feel like I had the horrible stench washed off my skin. The air is filled with anger, hatred, and violence. A fog hangs over the area, dispirited, hopeless.

I also don't want to get her hopes up. The possibility the killer is already present is slim. The timeline for the deaths and when Wilson was arrested may rule out his involvement. However, we don't have hard and fast dates on the victims, so I already have hope. From what I remember of Wilson, he likes to talk, likes to brag. He's already in prison and I can dangle an imaginary carrot in front of him, make him believe if he tells me something of value, I can get him perks like cigarettes, or an extra hour in the exercise yard.

The watch goes in my desk drawer and I mentally prepare for the trip. There's more than Wilson in there because of my testimony. The warden is a brash fellow and not one of my biggest fans, but he has granted me a fifteen minute interview.

It could make or break my day. Hopefully, I can use my Jedi mind trick and maximize that time.

I grab my coffee and briefcase, ready to head out before Meg arrives. I leave a note on her art table about the files I've requested and the excuse of Juanita's search for her biological father as the reason for my absence from today. Odds are, she'll text before I'm on the freeway.

Once I'm at the prison, I'll have to notify JJ. He'll be pissed I didn't get his okay beforehand. All part of the plan to make sure he doesn't bum a ride as well. The last thing I need is to be in the car with him for a three and a half hour trip each way.

I almost make it out the back door unseen. I'm contemplating stopping at home to grab another watch when I hear Meg's keys in the lock. "Shit," I say under my breath, making a quick turnabout and nearly spilling my coffee as I sprint down the hall toward the front. My new heels are not easy to run in and I nearly trip.

She'll ask too many questions; demand answers I don't want to give. As I punch the security button and try to unlock the door quickly, the strap of my briefcase slides off my shoulder. It whacks the plant sitting just inside the door, nearly toppling it. I snatch the plant and juggle a coffee cup, another creative curse escaping my lips.

"Charlie?" Meg's voice rings out down the hallway. "Are you okay?"

Of course she knows it's me. She saw my car in the back parking lot. Escape is futile.

"Fine," I reply. Time is definitely not on my side today. "Just checking the security alarm."

I check it on a regular basis, so this won't raise suspicions. The plant looks a little lopsided and there's a small bit of dirt on the floor to clean, but I'm not wearing my coffee, so there's that.

"Are you dodging me?" I turn to find her behind me holding my note. She eyes my briefcase and travel mug.

"What? Of course not." I point toward the note. "I'm heading to West Virginia about a lead."

It's not a lie, exactly, leaving out the specifics of the trip. I watch her face, waiting to see if she believes this is about Miss Jones.

Her jaw sets. She knows I'm not telling the whole truth. "You should wait for JJ. He'll be here in a few minutes."

"JJ?" My pulse picks up. "Why would he go with me to investigate a lead for Juanita Jones?"

Meg balls up the note and throws it at me. "He came by this morning looking for you, and he told me about Mickey Wilson."

The floor seems to shift under my feet. I'm baffled. Is JJ reading my mind these days?

I share a duplex with my sister, we each have our own side. Meg needs more privacy than I do, but I have more secrets—at least, I think I do—so it suits us well. We're together almost 24/7, and it works for us, but we need time alone. Besides, she likes to watch public television. Kill me now. I'm more of a *Law and Order* fan.

My sister senses my confusion, the wheels turning in my head, trying to find a way out of this. "I mentioned our break-through to him last night. He said you'd want to talk to Mickey."

He put two and two together. I'm pissed she told him, but also slightly relieved. At least he isn't reading my mind. "I wanted to get an early start and didn't want to bother you. You have things to do here, and Wilson is most likely a dead end."

She doesn't argue, just nods once. "You shouldn't go alone."

"I work well alone."

All she does is blink, but I know I've said the wrong thing. "I meant—"

One hand rises. A stop sign. "I know, Charlie. Going inside a federal prison to talk to a serial killer isn't my thing. You're protecting me again, and I appreciate it, but you don't have to lie. Oh look, JJ just pulled in."

She gives me an evil smile before turning on her heel and heading back to her office.

I feel like the villain in an old time movie, foiled again.

JJ bangs on the front door, making me jump. I take my time setting my coffee and briefcase on Haley's desk before letting him in.

He checks his watch, the giant, expensive Rolex that never loses time or dies. "You ready? We're wheels up in twenty."

"What are you talking about? I'm headed to Hazelton."

He grins. "I commandeered a helicopter. I'll have you there and back in no time."

Why am I not surprised? JJ has unlimited resources, people who owe him favors. "I'm not spending taxpayer money on this. It's probably a waste of time."

"You have to follow every lead, don't you, Charlie? That's what I like about you, your thoroughness. Just so happens I need to run an errand to the penitentiary anyway."

"Is that so?" He's a slick liar. "In regard to what?"

He taps on his cell and holds the screen for me to see. "I'm on a committee handling the Federal Bureau of Prisons' use of restrictive housing for inmates with mental illness. I need to speak to Warden Delacruz about a couple line items in his audit and bring back files for my boss."

This man. He makes magic happen and it infuriates me, even when it makes my life easier. "I appreciate the offer but I'm driving."

JJ shrugs, as it makes no difference to him. "No point in you going at all then. I'll interview Wilson and be back before you even get there."

The grip on my coffee cup is getting too tight. I may still end up with stains on my new shoes before this day is over.

Throwing the cup at JJ's smirking face holds appeal. I restrain myself and look for the silver lining. At least in the helicopter, small talk will stay limited to the case. The noise will require headphones and the pilot will be able to hear anything we say. The quick turnaround is an advantage too. I'll be home before lunch, and able to at least confirm whether Wilson has anything to do with the two skulls in Meg's office.

Underneath all of that, I realize I'm slightly relieved I don't have to go alone. I don't need JJ with me, but I like the idea that he'll make the process smoother with Delacruz and be a second pair of ears to listen in on my interview with Wilson. It always helps to have him to bounce ideas off of. JJ is brilliant as well as sexy and annoying. He can frame things in his mind, like cases and criminals, much like I do as a profiler and psychologist. But he always brings new insight to any case I've worked.

Meg clears her throat, announcing her presence. "Don't forget to FaceTime me when you get there."

"Why?"

"I want to hear what this guy says. Wear your earbud thingy so I can have you ask him questions, if I have any."

"Why don't you come along?" JJ asks. "There's room in the helo, and you can hear what this asshole has to say in person."

"What?" I nearly come out of my shoes. "Meg hates this kind of stuff. It makes her sick."

"Yes, it does." She nods, but I see a light in her eyes. "But I just might take you up on the offer, Mr. U.S. Attorney."

"No." I pull myself up to my full height. "Meg, this is way out of your comfort zone. Way out of your skill set."

"Either I go, or I stay here and make myself crazy working on reconstructions." She gives me a look that says it all. If I don't want to worry about her obsessing here, I'll have to take her with me. "At least if I go, I'll get out of the office and feel like I'm accomplishing something."

I sigh. Arguing with her is a waste of time. Ditto JJ. "Don't get your hopes up. I'll do my best with this guy, but this could be a crazy lead that doesn't pan out."

My sister walks up to me, removing the watch from her wrist and handing it over. "You wouldn't be heading to that prison if you didn't believe there's value in it. I'll go too, and we'll keep each other balanced."

The metal of her watch is still warm from her skin as I slip it on my wrist. Time is definitely not on my side, but my sister is, and the hope I see in her eyes is all I need.

I turn to JJ. "What are you waiting for? Let's go."

His grin broadens and he rushes us out the door.

7

MEG

*P*risons give me the creeps.

I realize I'm not special in this regard, but I remind myself of that little factoid as our driver pulls through the gate of Hazelton Penitentiary, a maximum security facility that doesn't feel the need to soften the name by using *Institution* or *Complex*.

It's a prison, through and through. Complete with coiled barbed wire on top of high fences and a guarded surveillance tower that reminds occupants their every move is monitored.

Every.

Move.

The driver leaves us at the entrance where we enter a brick building and are met by an officer waiting behind sealed glass. Before we arrived, JJ gave us the rundown, so I know it's bullet-proof. The thought closes in on me, leaves me aching to turn around and stick my head out the door for fresh air. Like I said, prisons give me the creeps. Our credentials are checked, and we're given visitors passes before being escorted down a long hallway where a guard opens a steel gate. We're searched and our briefcases scanned by a metal detector. It's airport security on steroids here.

Once we're cleared, I take up the rear and follow Charlie, JJ, and yet another guard through yet another set of steel doors. The guard, Dan, according to his name tag, is a big guy. Maybe six feet with broad shoulders and a cocky walk that's probably more survival than representation of his personality. When spending five days a week with homicidal maniacs, a commanding presence would be a requirement.

The long, white-walled hallway carries a stench of staleness. As if fresh air hasn't made its way through since the day the building was enclosed. Which, in fact, it probably hadn't. Prisons, after all, weren't meant to be pleasant, breathable places.

We're ushered through a heavy door that swings closed behind us, the ker-thunk echoing throughout the corridor. The further we go into the bowels of the building, the more my nerves jump. My shoulders are already bunched nearly to my ears and I grit my teeth. It's simply not a natural state. More than that, I hate the weakness that comes with the absolute shredding of my nervous system because I'm somewhere I despise.

Prisons and hospitals. Not good places.

The three of us remain quiet, dutifully following our escort through another maze of hallways and solid steel doors until he finally stops.

Before unlocking the door, Dan turns to us. "We've got him in there already."

Judging by the creases in his skin, he can't be more than forty, but for the first time, I notice his hair is already graying. Another result of the job, I'm sure.

"I'll wait out here," JJ says.

We discussed this on the ride over. Three visitors would be overkill. Plus, Charlie intended on getting information from

Mickey regarding four unsolved murders. Having the United States Attorney present might give our interviewee a case of locked lips.

Dan nods then turns his attention to Charlie and me. "We'll be right here. Mickey isn't usually a problem, but he's shackled for your safety. While you're in there, the door will be unlocked. When you're ready come out."

"Thank you," Charlie says. "We shouldn't be long. If he's not forthcoming, we won't be staying."

Dan shoves his key into the lock, and I steady myself. Unlike my sister, I haven't spent a lot of time with cold-blooded killers. I don't have the constitution for it. The few times I've been forced to be in the presence of animals like Mickey Wilson, I seem to absorb their rancid energy and it puts me in a funk for days. It's as if they attach themselves and I can't shake them loose.

Which is why I usually leave this stuff to Charlie. This time though, I wanted to see this man. Look him straight in the eye. For Emily.

For Avery.

Dan swings it open and I follow Charlie inside. The white-haired man is chained to the table, but he angles his rail thin upper body toward us. In the photo Charlie showed me on the ride here, Mickey's hair was dark brown. It must've been from years ago because this guy in front of me looks ready for the Early Bird special at the local diner.

This skinny, white-haired old man butchered all those women?

He gives Charlie a long once over. Have I mentioned my sister is beautiful? Her light brunette hair combined with hazel eyes and high cheekbones make her, even at her worst, an absolute stunner. Mickey appreciates this, ogling her with hungry eyes that scream of evil. God only knows what he'd do to her outside these walls.

Protocol aside, no wonder they have him shackled.

"Well," he says, "my lucky day. You're my second visitors, and you're so much more enticing. What do you think, sweetheart? Want to show me your tits?"

And, here we go.

"Knock it off, Mickey." Charlie, ever the cool, professional, offers him her nothing face. The flat-lipped, you're-an-idiot one. "I wasn't willing the last time you asked, what makes you think that's changed?"

His mouth lifts into a half-smile. "Thought you'd take mercy on a locked up old man. Can't blame me for trying."

Um, actually, we can.

Opposite Mickey, there are two chairs tucked under the table. Charlie pulls one out and motions for me to sit. "This is my...associate."

My sister. Always protecting me.

I nod and wait for Charlie to set her briefcase on the floor before sitting down. Once seated, she retrieves the red folder containing case notes and my sketch of Avery. She sets it on the table and takes a second to straighten the folder. As expected, the pause lures Mickey's narrow-eyed and extremely focused gaze. My sister is no dummy. She knows how to work a situation. She also understands the inner-workings of a psychotic mind and right now, a depraved serial killer sits across from her, damned curious about what might be inside.

But Charlie is in no hurry. She sits back and crosses her long legs, placing her hands in her lap. Her interview pose. Casual, but firm.

"I'm working a cold case," she says, her voice direct and unflinching. "I think you might be able to provide background."

The killer's eyebrows hitch. "Background?"

"Yes."

"Like what?"

"Like, you're already going to die in here and we have four

women, all young, all blondes, found near the beltway. I think, based on my prior interaction with you, you might know something about these murders."

Go. Charlie.

As usual, she's not taking any guff. She wants answers. So do I.

Mickey lifts a shoulder. "And what? You want me to tell you I killed them so you can provide—what's that word?"

He peers up at the ceiling and makes a humming noise that grates against my already compromised nerves. I know Charlie has a system, a routine, if you will, but this place and man are awful. It's as if someone has opened a valve and every last bit of my energy has drained.

After a full ten seconds, Charlie or no Charlie, I can't stand it anymore. "Closure."

My voice draws his attention and he stares at me. His eyes are a coffee brown dark enough to blur his irises, leaving nothing but two blots of blackness on his face. All is see is death. A shiver runs straight to my heels, but I remain still, refusing to let this filth know he's rattled me.

"Yeah," he says. "Closure."

Charlie waves an elegant hand. "Why not? You're not going anywhere, and it won't cost you anything."

"But maybe it'll get me something."

This we expected. We'd even discussed potential bartering items with JJ. During the conversation, he guided us on reasonable requests versus the hell-no variety.

Charlie maintains her pose, clearly unaffected by the fact she's sitting in front of a serial killer while I'd like to vomit. Given her experience, I'll leave the negotiating to her.

"What do you want?" She asks.

An odd glint fills Mickey's eyes and my stomach twists. I'm no psychologist, but my sister stirs something in him, and it scares the crap out of me.

He leans in a bit and nudges his chin at her. "A look at your tits."

Again with this? For the love of God, if it would get him to admit what he did, I'd show him mine. They're bigger than Charlie's anyway.

I let out a mental sigh and Charlie gives me the side-eye, the one that tells me I'm screwing up her interview. Perhaps that sigh wasn't mental. I sit back and press my lips together, determined to stay quiet and let my sister do her thing.

Flashing her tits at Mickey falls in JJ's hell-no requests, I'm sure. Charlie's as well. "If I recall correctly," she says, "you're a smoker."

"Yeah. No joy in it anymore. Can't get my brand in here. I gotta go with the shit they bring in."

Excellent.

Charlie nods. "How about I have the US Attorney speak to the warden? Maybe we can get you a couple cartons of your brand."

"Four."

Charlie cocks her head, offers a sultry smile that has that gleam in his eye sparking again. I really wish she wouldn't do that. Prisoner or not, I don't like the way he looks at her. As if he'd like to eat her flesh.

"Three," Charlie negotiates.

As much as I understand the unfolding power struggle, it irritates me. We have murdered women to identify and these two are playing games.

"No deal," Mickey says.

Dammit.

I grab the red folder and slide it toward me. *Fffftttt,* the card stock brushes against the table, the sound snapping the ruin known as my last nerve.

Charlie's head whips in my direction, but I ignore her warning glare. I'm done screwing around. He's toying with us. I

43

flip the folder open and dig through the small stack to the sketch I drew of Avery. Then I slap it in front of Mickey with a *thwack* that brings another sick smile to his lips. Yes, I've given him the upper hand by letting him see my lack of patience. Honestly, I don't care. I get to walk out of this hellhole while he's stuck.

So, who really has the power here?

Beside me, Charlie finally sets her hands on the table. She appears cool, always the ultimate professional, but I know my sister and I can feel the steam shooting from her pores.

Sorry, sis. I jab my finger against the sketch. "Her."

Mickey glances at the image. "What about her?"

"She's dead. One of the murdered blondes. She fits the profile of your victims. Did you kill this woman?"

8

CHARLIE

*M*y sister has hijacked my interview with a serial killer.

I want to give her my *stop talking* face, but that would require I glance at her a third time, and if I do, Mickey will know how frustrated I am. *Never let them see you sweat.*

"We're waiting, Mickey," I say.

I reach down and pinch Meg's thigh–*let me handle this*. She flinches slightly, but she knew it was coming so it's no surprise. We used to pinch each other under the dinner table all the time.

I dangle the carrot in front of the killer again. "Answer and I'll get your cigarettes."

The sketch of Avery is good—my sister's work is always exceptional, and it blows me away. How she can take a skull and bring it to life gives me chills.

Mickey throws a look at the sketch, then scrutinizes it more closely. He sits forward and–*yep, there it is*—I can tell by the twitch in the left corner of his mouth he recognizes the face. He stares at the girl's eyes and his breathing grows faster, shallower.

My stomach sinks at his obvious tells. Damn. She's one of his.

At least this victim and her family may get closure after all.

"Who is she?" I tap the picture, bringing Mickey's attention back to the present, instead of the past attack he is mentally reliving. Bastard. "How did you find her? Why did you target her?"

One of his nicotine-stained fingers touches her hair, brushes across the lips. "My sweet, sweet Tonya. You were quite the fighter, weren't you?"

Meg stiffens, gripping the seat of her chair. I know she's battling the urge to slap Mickey's hand away.

I'm doing the same. "Tonya who? I need a last name."

His finger slides down the poor girl's jawline to the base of her throat. "Don't remember, but what I do remember is the way her pretty blue eyes bugged out when I put my thumbs *right here.*"

He starts to demonstrate, and I know Meg will come out of her seat if he does, so I pull the sketch away and slam my fist on the table, startling them both. "Why her, Mickey? Tell me or the interview is over."

He shrugs it off, once more slouching in his chair and looking at me with hard eyes. I don't miss the way his gaze drops to my throat before he sighs audibly. "You know why."

"I want to hear you say it."

I feel Meg's scalding look—she probably wonders why I don't list the identifying common denominators to speed this up. But I want *him* to confirm the details. You never give a criminal the facts, you make him admit them on his own.

"Come on, Agent Schock, or is it Dr. Schock? I never could keep that straight—you're a Fed, a psychologist...wait, you're a bitch. Maybe that's what I should call you. You know my profile as well as anyone. You know why I killed those girls." He leans forward again, flashes a cunning smile. "You know why you're really *not* my type."

"My partner is not familiar with your MO," I say offhand-edly, as if his smile isn't pure evil and makes my skin crawl. "I figure you want to fill her in. You always told me I didn't really understand you. If I detail your official profile, I'll probably get something wrong, won't I?"

His ego is far too big to not take the bait. Killers like him love to gloat and who does he have in this penitentiary that wants to listen?

He glances over at Meg, smug. "College girls, athletic, and blond. Book smart but no common sense. They believe they're invincible, go running by themselves at night or are too busy looking at their phones instead of who might be in the dark parking lot when they leave the bar. You know the type. Lots in D.C., always pretending to be so important. Tonya was one of them, perfect body, running by herself at night in Hollings Park. It was all too perfect, too easy, to snatch her and show her just how insignificant she was."

Hollings Park. Only half a mile from the Beltway.

"So it's about power for you?" Meg doesn't miss a beat. "Feeling superior?"

At least she didn't ask about the absence of rape. I'm proud of her for not giving up that detail, which is vital since Mickey here couldn't get it up unless he killed them first. Luckily, he wasn't into necrophilia.

I fill Meg in on a bit of Mickey's history. "Mickey had an abusive mother, and took it out on his sister's dolls, decapi-tating them with his bare hands. Mommy forced him to sleep in their locked basement, told him no woman would ever love him—he goes for the throat of his victim as an act of shutting up his mother."

"The bitches deserved what they got," Mickey replies, shooting me a glance since I fall into the 'bitch' category. He

47

taps his thumb on the table. "Interview is over. I want my cigarettes."

The door opens and Dan, the guard, steps in with three cartons of Marlboros. He sets them down as I give him a questioning look. "Complements of the US Attorney," he says.

JJ strikes again. How in the world he came up with them in the time I've been sitting here is beyond me. He's probably already figured out Tonya's last name and notified the detectives in charge of her case.

Lyrics from an old Heart song swim through my brain. *He's a magic man.*

I give Mickey my best hardass glare and place my hand on the cartons when he reaches for them, pulling them back toward me. "One more thing. We have another sketch to show you."

I nod at Meg. She pulls the one of Emily from the folder. I can see my sister holding her breath as she spins it for Mickey to see. "What about her? Did you kill her too?"

Mickey's eyes narrow before he glances away. "Do I get more if I answer?"

I smile. "I can make it happen, but you have to tell the truth. If you lie, I'll know, and then not only will you *not* get extra, I'll throw these in the trash."

He wants the cigarettes so bad he's almost salivating, but his tell is missing—no twitch, no smirk, no change in his breathing–when he glances at Emily again.. "Yeah, her too. "

"Name?" I question.

He scratches his ear, makes a face. "Mary? Ann? Jane? I don't recall, but I do remember killing her."

"Where? Did you find her at the park like Tonya?"

He shrugs. "Sounds about right."

"You're lying," Meg says. "You never saw this girl, and you certainly didn't kill her."

She may be an artist, but she's got the instincts of a profiler.

I remove the boxes and rise from my chair. "You're right, Mickey, this interview is over."

His shackles jangle as he lunges for me, the evil look firmly in place once more. "You goddamn bitch!"

I hustle Meg to the door and throw a smile at Mickey. "It's *Dr.* Goddamn Bitch to you."

9

MEG

I don't know what it is about Thursday, but lately I can't seem to stay on schedule.

Today, the morning after the Mickey visit that left me with a sleepless and extremely creeped out night, I'm exhausted. Emotionally and physically drained to the point where hours of meditation won't help.

And, I started the day with a call from my mother.

My parents live in Cedarwood Cove, Maryland, a small town an hour out of D.C. where Charlie and I grew up. Mom had big news to share. Apparently, skeletal remains had been found along the Silver Tail, a hundred mile long river that flows through our hometown.

For Mom, that equals a barrel—possibly two—of catnip. Before Charlie and I barged into her world, Mom was a journalist for the Annapolis Capital. It was a role she cherished, absolutely thrived on, but gave up to be a stay-at-home mom. As grateful as I am that she was home each day and always available, she shouldn't have given up her career. Even as a kid, I sensed something in her. A loss I didn't quite understand until I became an adult.

Not that she'd been a bad mother. She's great. Rock-solid in all the ways one should be. Even if she took the PTA president to task over a bake sale that somehow discriminated against boys.

Hey, I never said she wasn't nuts.

As honorable as sacrificing her career had been, there was a hunger within her that couldn't be satisfied by life as a stay-at-home mom. I sensed an emotional void in her. That down deep she really didn't want to be home. She may have been there physically, but I needed more. I needed to talk to her about... whatever...boys, my friends, things bothering me, the color of the sky and why I loved it and she always seemed preoccupied. Studying the newspaper for stories she could've written, corruption cases she could have chased. Murderers she may have helped catch. Even when Mom was home she wasn't present. She'd be deep in her journal making notes about Gayle, our neighbor across the street.

That hunger still exists and manifests itself by her spying on Gayle, who keeps odd hours. Dad used to joke that a man with that name had to be out all night because during the day too many people tormented him for having a woman's name.

Suspicious of said hours, Mom started watching him. Keeping an eye out, as she'd say.

And taking notes.

In her mind, Gayle could have been up to anything. Weapons smuggling, drug trafficking, female slavery. When it came to him, my mother's imagination ran wild and fueled her need to dig, to find the truth. To this day, years later, she's still searching.

She has journals dedicated to his daily activities. When he came home, when he left, the day he cleared six garbage bags from his garage leaving Mom to think he could be disposing of a dismembered body.

She has no real proof of this, but the man's unusual

schedule ran headlong into her desire to have her career back and created the perfect storm of insanity.

So, on this Thursday morning, when skeletal remains were found on the banks of the Silver Tail, well, Mom called me, convinced it might be one of Gayle's victims.

At which point, I decided a trip to my hometown was in order before my mother ran to the cops with fifteen years' worth of journals and accused the quirky man of murder.

Talk about creating a problem with your neighbor.

It took Dad and I over an hour to convince Mom to hold off, to see where the investigation led before she approached law enforcement with her theories. By the time we were done, Dad looked as if he'd climbed Everest. He may have even sprouted a few extra gray hairs.

But, phew. Close one. She's as crazy as can be, but I love her. She's family and for me, that's what is most important. When things go south, the only people I know I can count on are my parents and Charlie. I think that's what drives me on these cold cases. If one of them went missing, I'd lose my mind. It would rip a chunk out of me I'd never get back.

When I think of Emily and all those lost kids from when I was in the sixth grade, that's what I feel. I could have been one of those kids and their families have no idea where they are. I can't live with that.

It is, in fact, my greatest fear and I hope to never experience it. Even thinking about it gives me jitters.

I kiss my parents goodbye, warn my mother to stay put, and leave my childhood home. Mom won't be put off for long, so I hop in my van and head straight to the police station. Charlie and I, given our work with cold cases, are minor celebrities in our little town. Letting the chief know I'd be willing to help if the remains went unidentified will give me access and an ability to keep my mother in check by telling her the investigation is active. At the very least, I could create a composite sketch.

The chief was out at the site, but I left a message with his assistant to have him call me. While in town, I make a quick detour to the Silver Tail. Not so much to nose around, but to visit my favorite rock. From what Dad told me, the body was found four miles downriver. Something I'm grateful for because over the years, this river—and the giant boulder I've claimed as mine—have given me countless hours of peace.

I deal with enough dead bodies in my day job, I don't need them littering my happy place. I know that sounds harsh, but I don't ask for a lot. When I'm here, it brings back happy thoughts from before the sixth grade when we played in the shed our dad built. The minute I hear the babble of the river, my stress level drops.

I pull into the makeshift lot. It was never meant to be a parking area, but years of folks driving over it has left nothing but hardened dirt and gravel. I feel the crunch of pebbles under my tires and my body damn near sighs. *My place.*

I lock my doors and head toward my spot. The air is warm and moist, and I take a second to center myself. To block out murders, dead bodies, and cold cases. If I lived closer to my hometown, I'd come out here every day and meditate.

Just ahead is the she-shed Dad made for us when we were kids. He needed approval from the zoning board for the single room wood structure and after six months of negotiating finally agreed the town's nature center could use the dwelling for various events. To date, I'm not sure they ever actually used it, but Charlie, me, and our friends sure did.

I wind my way along, loving the feel of my soft-soled shoes moving over grass and patches of dirt. Beside me, the river is low from a lack of rain and piled rocks break the surface. On summer days, I've been known to kick off my shoes and wade right in. Not today. No time and it would be cold. There's nothing relaxing about that.

But there's my rock. A boulder actually, big enough for two people to share. I've never brought anyone here though. The most I've done is point it out to Charlie, but she's not about to ruin her silk clothing by sitting on a dirty old rock.

I pause and close my eyes, absorbing the rustle of swaying leaves and chirping birds. The sun's heat warms me, and my body responds by releasing the tightness in my shoulders.

My rock. I open my eyes and climb across several smaller boulders that lead to the river's edge. I check my footing as I go, testing the stability of each before stepping on it. I've learned the hard way that slipping will win me a concussion or various scraps and cuts.

Then I'm there, standing in my happy place as water flows beneath. I avoid the sharp edges of granite that'll dig into my skin then settle into my favorite crossed legged position. If I wanted, I'd hang my feet over and my toes, even with the lack of rain, would skim the water.

My place.

I give myself ten minutes to block out the world then another three to return to reality.

I say a short prayer for the person—the decomposed body —found just miles from here. I don't know what the circumstances around that death were, but I hope it was peaceful. I've already told Charlie when it's my time, I want her to bring me here. I don't care if they have to roll me out here on a hospital bed, this is my only request. To die in my happy place.

On my rock.

Plenty of time for that though. Now I'm preoccupied with these murders and need to get to the office.

My morning is shot. That's all I can think as I drive and contemplate the work to be done before I leave tonight. The lack of my sister's BMW and Matt's SUV will help. No distractions. Charlie had mentioned something last night about being gone. Court maybe. Or to see that ancestry client she picked up from JJ. I'm not sure. I was focused on the curve of Avery's cheek at the time and Charlie's words were lost. It's an issue with me. Charlie knows it. If my knowing where she would be this morning was that important, she'd tell me *and* text me.

And yes, it's still Avery. The lead was a bust. Charlie went crazy yesterday trying to find a missing Tonya that matches our gal. No dice so far, and she and JJ ruled out all the cold cases in this area that might be linked to Mickey. Not one missing college girl with blond hair named Tonya in the three-state region. Either that bastard Mickey lied, or Tonya didn't tell him her real name. Good for her.

Matt? Who knows where he is? Charlie handed off some cases and he disappeared. Matt's the brother we never had so we don't stress about his vanishing acts. His work ethic rivals Charlie's so we don't need him to check in every day. There are cases where he's worked twenty-four hours straight. No sleep. At all. That's the guy he is.

How he and my sister have the energy for what they do, I'll never know. Then again, they say the same about me.

I park my well-used minivan in my usual spot. The banged-up vehicle makes my sister cringe but it has plenty of cargo space for my supplies and it's been paid off for five years. Why do I need a snazzy new one? I'd rather spend that money searching for victims.

After locking it, I walk the few steps to the door, shove my key in and turn it. Or at least try to. There is no *cha-chunk* from the heavy deadbolt which means...

Unlocked.

Hunh. I step inside, shut the door again and flip the bolt. We're not freaks about the doors, but we've been around crime enough to know we're a whole lot safer when they're locked.

Particularly with what we do. Who knows when the

disgruntled spouse of a client may want to have a chat about the naughty pictures Schock Investigations took?

"Haley?"

Our office assistant appears at the end of the hallway. Separating us are four doorways. The conference room, my studio, and Charlie and Matt's offices.

"Good morning," she says.

"Morning." I point over my shoulder. "The door was unlocked."

"Oh, shoot." She clunks herself on the head. "I'm sorry. UPS delivered your supplies and the phone blew up. By the time I got done, he was gone, and I forgot to lock up."

"It's all right."

Fresh out of college, Haley is determined to do a good job. We're probably an entry-level stepping stone for a pretty twenty-two-year-old with a psychology degree, but I can't blame her for the fact we'll more than likely lose her in a year. She's only been with us four months, but she's good. Conscientious, punctual, and doesn't mind grunt work mixed in with the not-so-grunt.

"I had Jack put the boxes in your studio."

Did I mention she's on a first name basis with all the delivery guys? They love her. She hands them coffee and they put the packages wherever she wants. The fact she's a tall blond with a face I'm dying to sculpt doesn't hurt.

"Thank you," I say because when you get boxes and boxes of art supplies, it's nice to have someone else carry them for you.

"Do you need me to unpack them?"

"No. Thanks. I'll take care of it."

I find said boxes neatly stacked in the corner of my office by the closet. There's nothing pressing in there, so I add unloading them to my mental to-do list for the day.

Silence descends on my sanctuary and after the wacky

morning I've had, I pause for a second and close my eyes. I inhale then release the breath, allowing my brain a few brief seconds of rest. A musky scent hangs in the air. UPS man Jack, I assume, laying the aftershave on a bit heavy. I'm not one for scented soaps and I wrinkle my nose, wishing for a window to crack open.

I turn to the stand where Avery waits. "Good morning," I say. "Plenty to do today."

A flash of white catches my eye and I glance to the far corner. Something churns inside me and I feel a burst. Like a pilot light that won't fire, and I hate it.

"Haley!"

The flame inside finally ignites and the initial paralyzing shock melts away. I'm on the move, heading straight to Emily.

"What is it?"

Haley's voice is breathy, rushed. I scoop up the soft, honey blond wig sitting on the floor and point to the harsh platinum one on Emily's head.

"What happened here?" My voice is clipped, teetering on the edge of control.

I should check that, but...no. Haley's been an employee long enough to know I don't like my work touched. At all.

She's also aware of my obsession—yes, I'll admit it—with Emily. The fact that someone has come in here, into *my* space, and touched her drives me nearly insane.

Has she not suffered enough? Murdered, left in the cold like trash for years and now this?

Haley's mouth opens, forming a silent *oh*. "I...I don't know. It's the first I'm seeing it."

Resisting the urge to touch the ugly platinum wig, I set the honey blond on my work table, push past Haley and head to Charlie's office. "Was Jack the only one in there?"

Haley follows me, her long legs easily keeping pace. "As far as I know. I got here at eight forty-five and the alarm was still on."

"What time did Jack arrive?"

"Um, around ten-thirty, I think. You don't believe he...?"

She thinks? Excellent.

I flip the light on in Charlie's office and note my twitching hands. The rage is streaming now, all that roiling emotion flooding my brain. I remind myself to stay calm. To focus. Whoever touched Emily, I'll get the bastard.

I know this because we have 24/7 video surveillance.

"It couldn't have been Jack," Haley says. "Why would he do that?"

"I don't think it is."

"Then who?"

"I don't know, but we're about to find out."

I roll Charlie's chair to the credenza along the far wall and sit while waiting for her desktop for the security system to boot up.

After logging in, a few keystrokes bring me to this morning's videos. I find the one for the hallway camera and click on it. A second later, a color image pops up, the timestamp showing 12:00:01.

Thinking logically, if someone had broken in, the alarm would've sounded. Plus, Haley just told me she'd disarmed it when she arrived. Somewhere between then and now, someone screwed with my Emily.

I select the small circle on the video bar until it reaches 8:43:00. I slow my clicking down, moving at one minute intervals until I get to 10:30:00. No Jack.

Click, click, click.

Click.

I keep going. Another ten and there's Haley, hustling to the back where she pauses, obviously asking who it is. Good girl. She opens the door and our delivery man enters with two boxes he sets in my office. Haley signs for it, points to the reception area and Jack nods. He watches for a second as she jogs away from him, her ankles wobbling on her high-heels. Haley disappears from view and Jack exits, returning a minute later with two more boxes.

Then he's gone. 10:46:35.

And the door is unlocked.

I click another dozen or so times, searching for anyone else who may have entered.

Bingo. 10:51:13.

The back door comes open. A man in jeans, a black sweatshirt, a black baseball cap and one of those reflective vests utility workers are required to wear stands in the doorway, peering straight ahead. I zoom in as tight as the system will allow and see the chin-length platinum blond hairs that hangs below his cap.

A rush of adrenaline explodes, rushing straight down my neck and firing another burst of anger over the invasion of my space. I lock my teeth together. Bastard.

His head is dipped and there's a logo on the cap, but I can't make it out. That'll be a job for Charlie or Matt. They have techie contacts that might be able to get a tighter zoom. For now, it's above my pay grade.

He lingers for a second, then another. Waiting, I presume, to see if someone might appear to question him.

Behind me, Haley gasps.

I've pretty much forgotten she's there and I peer up at her.

"Oh, my God," she says. "I'm so sorry."

I pause the video. She's *sorry*? She could've been murdered and *she's* apologizing to *me*.

"Don't you dare apologize. I'm just glad you're all right. Do you want to watch this? Maybe you shouldn't."

"Oh, I'm watching. That way if I see the fucker, I can kick him in the balls."

Ha. I like her spunk. She reminds me of my sister.

I click once more and the video rolls. "All right then."

Our intruder moves through the hallway, his steps light but quick. The conference room door is closed, but he pauses. He keeps his head low with the bill of his cap hiding his features as he presses his ear against it. Then he spots the next door—my studio—open and peels away. In three strides, he reaches my office and peeps in, sees the space empty, then enters.

At this moment, while I watch some stranger invade my sanctuary, I regret the war I waged when Charlie suggested security cameras for each office. I threw every ounce of my being into the argument. I'm an artist, I told her. I can't work with cameras spying.

Now I wish I'd let my security conscious sister have her way.

Haley and I sit quietly. What is there to say when a strange man creeps around two doors from where she fields calls?

I look at her and my gaze locks on her blond hair and the long column of her neck. The weight of a full-on body slam hits me. This could have been so much worse. I could've returned to find our assistant with her throat slashed clear to the bone.

"Jesus," I finally say.

"It's crazy," she replies. "This guy has the nerve to just walk in."

I shake my head and refrain from telling her he could be a serial killer. Because, really? Why else would he be in my studio putting a blond wig on Emily right after we determined we have a serial killer with an obsession for blondes?

Less than a minute later, the camera catches the bill of the cap as the man pokes his head out. I am frozen, my gaze glued to the screen as more of him is revealed. Slowly, an inch at a time, his entire head, the one suddenly lacking blond hair, comes into view. He keeps his chin dipped, obscuring his face, but from this angle, I can't see any hair.

He once again checks the length of the hall—all clear—and

steps from my office. He moves casually, as if he didn't just invade my personal space and defile my work.

Seconds later, he makes his exit and my rage spews again. Not only has he touched Emily, he came insanely close to Haley, our young, very pretty, and very blond assistant.

10

I'm interviewing Yvonne Wagner, Juanita's biological mother, when I get a 911 text from Meg.

We had a break in. I think the killer knows we're looking for him.

She sent a photo, and I stare in confusion at the wig on the skull. I have to read the message three times before it sinks in.

...killer knows we're looking for him.

Holy crap.

"Is everything okay?" Yvonne is in her early sixties, her dishwater blond hair hiding the gray strands, her plump face showing very few wrinkles for her age. She insists she is Juanita's mother, and that the father was Polish.

"Fine." I fake a smile, trying to figure out how to excuse myself without blowing this meeting.

Yvonne's baby was illegitimate, and the father, Roland Kolosky, wasn't cut out for domestic life with a wife and child. He was in the Army and stationed overseas constantly—he was told about the pregnancy and wanted her to end it. She refused, but her parents forced her to give the baby up for adoption.

Apparently her aunt and uncle's hotel secretly catered to young, unwed mothers in the 1970s. Without saying it, Yvonne has hinted at the fact the mothers often turned over their babies to her aunt and uncle for private adoptions.

Private, *illegal* adoptions. There were two others who gave birth the same night, if her memory serves. All three were giving their babies up. What are the odds Juanita was switched with another baby that night?

Juanita should have her DNA tests back by now, but I haven't heard from her. The records of her birth are sketchy, and if there's no physical link, it solves this mystery while opening another—who are her real biological parents?

I thank Yvonne and rise, not finishing the tea she made for me. "I'm sorry, but something's come up. I have to run. Have you ever taken a DNA test?"

"Juanita wants me to," she says, "but I haven't yet. It's so..." She gives a shudder and plays with her cup.

"They're easy and quick. Would you be willing if I bring it by and walk you through it?"

She shrugs. "I know she's mine, so I'm not sure what it'll prove."

Surely after meeting Juanita this woman can see her genes aren't European Caucasian. People see what they want, I guess. Perhaps after finding her daughter—at least who she *thinks* is hers–after all these years, she's afraid of losing her again. "I'll be by tomorrow with a kit."

I say a hasty goodbye and text Meg that I'm on my way. *Be there shortly.*

Except I find JJ in Yvonne's driveway, leaning on my car. "What are you doing here?"

His arms are crossed, his suit jacket bunching around his broad shoulders. "Juanita told me you'd be here, and I was in the neighborhood."

Right. He's six miles from his office, in a rundown suburb. I give him my resting bitch face. "I don't have time to chat." I shoo him away. "Meg needs me."

"My attorney is two blocks over," he says, sounding a touch cheeky as he proves he's telling some version of the truth. His fingers skim my arm. "He has news."

Lawyer. Divorce. My breath hitches, partly from his touch and because I once more feel hope.

Some of my friends have been through divorce proceedings that were strung out over a year or more. I know they take time and can be gutwrenchingly painful. JJ's wife is a high-profile entertainment lawyer who doesn't want to give up her US attorney husband. That their divorce has topped the two-year mark shouldn't surprise me, but it still bugs the shit out of me. I want him for myself, dammit. "That's great." I reach for the car door. "I have to go."

He opens it for me before I can do it and helps me inside. He leans on the frame and says, "Can I call you later?"

I smell his intoxicating aftershave and see those baby blues —frank, with a touch of yearning in them. He's asking permission for once, instead of just doing whatever he wants. I want to grab him and hug him. Reassure him his lawyer has the news we've both been waiting for. "Good luck with the meeting," is all I say instead before forcing him out of the way as I shut the door.

He stands there for a moment, staring at me. I can't go anywhere until he moves his big SUV, so I hurriedly shoot off texts to Matt and a couple other beefy guys I know with IQs higher than mine—Justice "Grey" Greystone and Mitch Monroe.

I should mention to JJ about Meg's visitor, about the fear jabbing me under my breastbone, but I don't. Selfish me, I want him to go to that damn meeting. I want him to call me later and tell me Carlena Gage Carrington has signed the papers.

For now, I let him go and hope my other texts are answered. If a killer did pay us a visit, I'm going to need the other men in my life on board.

I don't make it home until after nine, having set up a whole new security system at the office. To be honest, calming Meg down took more effort than installing the cameras and motion sensors on all the doors and windows.

Hopefully, I impressed upon Haley the importance of never leaving the back door unsupervised. Especially now.

Grey and I went through all the footage and he's having his tech expert, Teeg, see if he can get a hit off our intruder's face, body shape, gait, or the logo on the cap. The blond wig on the skull is a blatant message if I've ever seen one. Matt is taking it to the FBI lab to have it tested to see if there are any cases using the same hair.

The biggest thing bothering me is how this guy—our suspected serial killer—found out we're investigating these cold cases. The request I put in to the various local police departments—did someone leak it? Or perhaps from the prison? Is this a killer employed by a law-enforcement agency?

The thought sends shivers over my skin.

I'm seconds from climbing into a warm bath and working through several possibilities when the doorbell rings. Meg doesn't use it or knock—she simply uses her key. Maybe it's Matt or Grey with some news.

Throwing on my robe, I check my phone and the app connected to the new front door camera. All I see is a hulking mass of a man with his head down, but I know that build, that brand of suit.

I rush to the door, tying the sash on the way. I'm annoyed and weirdly pleased when I find JJ on the doorstep looking like a million bucks.

A tired million bucks, but still sexy as hell, a five o'clock shadow heavy along his jawline. His big hands hold takeout bags. "I just heard about the break-in." He scans me from head to toe—checking that I'm in one piece or taking stock of my lack of clothing? —before coming back to meet my eyes. "Are you okay?"

I tighten the sash and realize it only serves to emphasize my suddenly perky nipples. *Traitors.*

That's what he does to me—instant insanity. My body betrays me even as my heart retreats. "Technically, it wasn't a break-in, the guy walked through the unlocked back door. I wasn't there when it happened, so yes, I'm fine, and no, I'm not up for company. I'll call you tomorrow."

Unless he has the news I've been waiting to hear...

He doesn't say anything, and I start to close the door feeling my hopes crashing down—if she'd signed, he wouldn't hesitate to tell me—and he strong-arms it. His look turns wounded. "You should have called me today."

She definitely did *not* sign the papers. "Everything's under control." *I hope.*

"You're dealing with a serial killer. He knows you're on his trail now and wants to play games with you and Meg. This is serious, Charlie."

"You think I don't know that?" I snort my frustration, not just at JJ, at the whole damn situation. "I installed an upgraded office security system, reprimanded our poor receptionist, interrogated the UPS guy, and have friends trying to match our visitor with known criminals in the area. Meanwhile, I've also added extra security around the duplex and tried to talk Meg into moving in with Mom and Dad until this blows over."

"Bet that went well." A small smile. He tips his chin to the other side of the duplex. "She's okay?"

"She's pissed and ready to go on a rampage, she just doesn't have a target."

"Can I see the video?"

"Why? Because you have ESP and will be able to figure out what the rest of us can't?"

Another wounded look. "Let me help. I brought dinner. I know you haven't eaten."

He knows me too well. My stomach growls as if on cue—another traitor. A part of me urges me to let him in, to show him the video, the photos I pulled from it, and to put him on follow-up duty with the police departments I contacted two days ago about the cold cases. Someone had to have leaked the info, alerting our killer.

But in reality, my body wants to invite him inside for ulterior purposes. It's been too long since our night together.

And it's not just my body that misses him.

I miss him. All of me.

Don't go there.

One of the things that's gotten me this far in life is selective risky behavior. It sounds counterproductive, and with my need for order and rules, it sometimes is. What I've found through the years is there are calculated risks worth taking, and those are what put me ahead of the class more times than not. I like to blame it on Meg's influence–she runs on emotion and that's always trouble. Truth is, I could stand to get out of my brain and trust my emotions more.

JJ is one big, fat, calculated risk. "How did the meeting go?"

His smile is tired. He knows what I'm referring to. "We're making progress."

The last bit of my hope dies.

My brain and heart feel torn to pieces, probably because there is no happy ending for us.

Unfortunately, that doesn't stop me from opening the door and letting him in.

I sense the conqueror in him doing a fist pump, the faintest hint of smugness in his smile.

"Don't get cocky. I have a lot of work to do tonight and, you're right, I haven't eaten. Pull out plates while I get dressed and pour me a glass of wine. My laptop is on the dining room table. The video is on there."

I plan to head to the bedroom to get dressed, but before I get two steps from the counter, he grabs my arm and draws me close. His arms go around me, and he pulls me into a tight hug.

It's suffocating and annoying, and oddly reassuring at the same time. I'm tired, freaked out a killer strolled into our offices in the middle of the day, and racking my brain to figure out how he knows we're investigating him. All that stops at the feel of JJ's arms around me.

His breath is warm on the top my head. "God, I'm glad you're okay."

My arms encircle his waist of their own accord to reassure him, my body melting into his bigger one. His expensive cologne is wearing off, but I can still find hints of sandalwood, mint, and cedar.

For me, that adds up to power and safety. Two of my favorite aphrodisiacs. I could stay like this in his arms, listening to his strong, solid heartbeat forever.

Nope.

Forever is not in the cards. I push away, and he reluctantly lets me go. "I've got to get dressed."

His hands hold onto mine as I try to make my escape. One finger slides over my pink topaz ring, wiggling it. "Not on my account."

There's something in his eyes, and it flips the switch. Just *boom*. Heat roars through me, and in less than a heartbeat, I'm in his arms again, his hands undoing the belt around my waist and opening the robe. Our mouths find each other, tongues dancing. My fingers grip the lapels of his shirt and the next thing I know, I hear buttons smacking into the counter, onto the tile floor. *Pop, pop, pop.* I free his muscled chest and press myself against that steady heartbeat once more.

My robe disappears, his hands tracing every inch of my

skin. He lifts me onto the countertop, the marble under my butt cold and unforgiving. This shocks me into reality, a sudden image of his wife's face burning in my brain.

"Stop." It takes all my willpower, but I push him away once more. Not easy to do since he outweighs me by a good eighty pounds. "We can't do this."

"Dammit." Soft, under his breath. He puts his hands in the air and steps back, one, two, three, as if he needs as much space as possible to keep himself from touching me. He only stops when he comes into contact with the fridge. Surprisingly, he doesn't argue. "I know. I'm sorry."

His face, his tone, say he's not sorry at all. He knows I jumped him, not the other way around. I hop off the counter, cheeks burning, and snatch my robe from the floor. "You better leave."

His voice comes out low, controlled. "If I promise not to touch you, can I stay?"

Promises, promises. I've made too many to myself that I've gone back on because of him.

I hate that my voice breaks when I answer. "I'm not kicking you out to...punish you." It's a lie, but the next thing isn't. "I just can't promise I won't touch you "—*attack you*—"if you stay."

A damning hint of a smile tickles his lips. "I could handcuff you to the chair."

Laughter bursts from my mouth. In this horrible situation, he reaches for humor.

And it works.

Stress, I tell myself. It's just the stress needing a release.

I don't know how to respond, everything in me riding a roller coaster of emotion, so I make a big deal out of putting my robe on and cinching it tight. "If you're staying, then you better get to work. Make me a plate of food, pour the damn wine, and watch the video."

I stomp off to my bedroom, and once inside, I hang my head

and let the breath I'm holding whoosh out of me. I grab my phone from my nightstand and text Meg with shaky fingers. She's the one player in this dynamic that'll keep me out of trouble.

JJ brought dinner. You better come over quick before he eats your share.

A moment later, she texts back.

Already ate.

Dammit.

I need you to go through the video with him. Tell him what happened.

She sends me a smiley face.

No dice, sis. You're on your own. Enjoy.

Enjoy?

I'm going to hell.

It takes a long moment before she sends another smiley face with her reply. My sister is an enabler.

It'll be worth it.

11

MEG

*A*fter a restless night, I stand in front of Avery's skull, a tissue depth marker in my hand. The vinyl nub resembles a pencil eraser and I can't resist rolling it between my thumb and forefinger. It's the first of many various depths I'll spend my day cutting then gluing to Avery's face. Or, at least what will eventually be her face. Until we have a positive ID on this woman, this supposed Tonya who Mickey claims to have murdered, she will still be Avery.

As with all humans, each skull has certain nuances—curves, angles, widths—and tissue depth markers help me determine how thick the clay needs to be in certain spots. All this information is provided by charts containing measurements for the anatomic points. By the end of the day, I intend to have all the markers labeled and placed in the areas they belong. Once they're all glued, I can begin the next part of the technical phase. That being placing prosthetic eyes and using the markers as a guide to begin sculpting with clay.

Mozart streams from my iPod dock and I close my eyes. Sometimes, the music settles me. Allows me to block out the myriad of office distractions—dinging emails, constantly ringing phones, Charlie and Haley's voices—so I can focus on the task at hand. With all the excitement from yesterday, it's most definitely a music day. Even if no one has arrived yet, there's an energy here, a foreign unease that gives me pause and forces me to continually shift my gaze to the door.

Our intruder has guaranteed one thing. I will never again work with my back to one.

I hate him for that. For making me feel vulnerable in a space I was previously comfortable in.

I glance at my watch. Seven forty-five. At any time Charlie will swoop in, calling out to me as she enters her office, dumps her briefcase, flips through yesterday's mail and listens to her messages while booting her laptop. She won't tell me about her night with JJ, acting like it never happened. All of this will be done with an elegant efficiency only my sister could pull off. She's a wiz that way. Unflappable. Me? I'd have crap strewn across my desk and my hair poking out in all directions while my mind exploded from the multitasking overload.

Mozart.

I tip my head back and breathe deeply. If Avery is to be identified, I have to shut out the noise. Focus and let intuition take over. When I'm in that zone, nothing gets between me and my subject. It's a stream of consciousness like no other. A high only attainable from the purity of working with my hands. No drug can deliver that.

Believe me, I've tried.

A few years back I got stuck on a reconstruction. It was as if my mind's eye refused to open. I became so tortured and paralyzed by my inability to work, an artist friend suggested I try a hallucinogenic he swore would enlighten my inner artist. At first, I balked. Then desperation set in and after a week of staring and making no progress, I called someone who provided me with what he referred to as a baby version of a methamphetamine known as Tik. I did as he instructed and wound up on the floor, wailing and vomiting. All while repressed thoughts of murder victims, skulls, and the corresponding emotions I've buried inside assaulted me, tore me apart with the force of a lion at feeding time and left me...gutted. Physically and mentally.

Welcome to my life.

Not my finest moment and a decision I regret to this day. No matter how many victims come through our doors, I have to protect myself. I have to learn regardless of the number of reconstructions I do, not all will be identified. I'm trying. I really am.

After that incident, I now rely on meditation—and an occasional pot brownie—to relax.

If Charlie knew about the latter, she'd lecture me for an hour. We all need something though. For her, it's JJ and his muscles. Me? CBD.

A chime sounds and my shoulders tense. The new alarm system has beeps, chimes, and gongs for just about every function. When the front door is opened, it beeps. Back door is a chime. Activating and deactivating involves loud gongs.

The whole thing is annoying and slices at my nerves like a saber, but Charlie has gone into precaution overload. I can't blame her. Not after the fear that gripped me when Haley could've been the next victim of a serial killer.

And we'd failed to protect her.

"Meg?"

Matt's voice. My shoulders unhunch and I curse yesterday's intruder. *Fucker.*

A second later, Matt pokes his head into my studio. "Whoa. What did I do?"

"What?"

"You called me a fucker."

Sighing, I toss the tissue depth marker into the small tray

on my worktable and silence Mozart. "Not you. The fucker that broke in yesterday."

Technically, he didn't. He walked right through the damned door.

"Ah," Matt says.

In his studious way, he fixes his blue gaze on Avery then slowly turns back to me. "When do you think you'll be done with her?"

Down deep, he also feels the pull. He just doesn't show it the way Charlie and I do. Matt doesn't speak of it, he simply does the work of hitting the street and asking questions. Digging until something pops.

"Barring any interruptions, maybe a week. Two at the most."

Silence once again descends, and I wait for him to meet my eye. He likes activity. Part of his coping mechanism I'm sure. Long stretches of quiet are definitely not his thing.

"Just heard from my guy at the FBI."

"The wig?"

He nods. "Yeah."

Damn. If Matt had good news, his excitement, like every other time he had pertinent info and couldn't wait to share, would've propelled him to call me on his way over.

"It's synthetic," he says.

This doesn't shock me. I've done enough reconstructions to recognize the differences between that and human hair wigs. Although the former have come a long way in recent years, the one I found on Emily had an unnatural shine to it, leading me to believe it was not only synthetic, but cheap as well.

"Let me guess," I say. "It came from a costume shop."

Matt shrugs. "Probably. No identifying labels. Without the person who purchased it—or a receipt—it's gonna be hard to run it down."

I know him too well. "But you'll try."

He smiles. "Of course. I pulled a list of all the party stores and costume shops in a sixty mile radius. Who knew there were so many of those suckers?"

"He also could have bought it online."

"Well, yeah, but I'm thinking it was an impulse thing. Even with overnight shipping, he'd have to wait. I'm going with him being too amped up for that. The idea came to him, he got har...er...pumped over it and hauled ass to the closest wig place. Either that, or he already had it. A prop or something."

Or something. I appreciate his attempt to clean up his language, but I don't have time for that. I want this investigation to be fast-moving and if that requires Matt, or anyone else to be painfully blunt, so be it.

"You can say he got hard. I've heard worse and we can't get hung up on propriety. Bigger battles to fight." I hold out my hands. "So, you're chasing down wigs. Can I do anything?"

"Not right now. Let me get into this. Maybe we'll get some video or a credit card receipt from the purchase. Any word from Teeg on a facial match?"

Teeg. The Justice Team's hacker extraordinaire and all-around tech genius. Personally, I suspect the super-secret black ops unit is an arm of the FBI, but no one will fess up and I sure as hell won't ask. All I know is they're our friends when it comes to providing intel. Grey and Charlie think alike and have similar personalities.

When Charlie told me Teeg was "running" our intruder's photo I didn't ask for details. Honestly, I don't care what government database he hacks into as long as we find this guy. "I don't think so. Charlie isn't in yet though."

The second the phrase leaves my mouth, a chime sounds. Back door.

Matt angles back, peeping down the hallway. "Speaking of."

"Hi," Charlie says, her voice coming closer and I picture her storming the hallway in her high heels. "I just heard from Teeg."

"And?" I ask, but my heart is already sinking. She's got the same look, the lack of excitement as Matt did a minute ago about the wig.

Poker face. "Nothing. We're still at square one. But don't worry, I have another idea."

I'm sure she does, but I still have the feeling she's only saying that to give me hope.

12

CHARLIE

I have six cold cases that fit our killer's parameters spread out on the conference room table. JJ strikes again. When he puts pressure on local law enforcement, they produce a lot faster than they do for me.

I spoke with Juanita this morning. Her results are back and show definite African American genes, a mixture from Ghana, Nigeria, and Somalia. I'm due at her mother's at three o'clock to help her with her DNA test.

Meg has been holed up in her art room all morning, her door shut and her music on. Shutting out me or the rest of the world?

I try not to take it personally, knowing she's as disappointed as I am Teeg came up with zero hits. So far, all my attempts to figure this out are a bust, and our killer's identity is too.

She hates the new security system and I don't blame her. All the bells and whistles are starting to get on my nerves too, and it hasn't even been twenty-four hours. Haley is jumpy too; I'm not sure if it's from what happened yesterday or the various alarms constantly going off.

My eyes flick to the tablet on my right, showing me different exterior views of our building. I see the back door, the front, both parking lots, and like the old-time Town Crier, I hear a voice in my head that says, *all is well.*

Unfortunately, the system has to stay. If nothing else, I need this constant surveillance and reassurance as much as I do the cases in front of me to keep my mind focused.

Them, along with Meg, Haley, Avery, and Juanita... they'll keep me from stewing over what happened last night with JJ. We ate, drank too much wine, watched the video a dozen times, and spit-balled different theories. We talked far into the night then did other things I'm not proud of, but even with a slight hangover, my body is far more relaxed than it has been in eons.

He's a magic man. I catch myself humming the old Heart song under my breath, after waking up to it playing in my head. It may not be classic Mozart, but it makes me smile for the first time today. I'm at war with myself, part of me feeling guilty about last night and the rest cheering like a kid on Christmas morning.

Guilt infuses my system once more, even as I keep humming. I pick up a file folder with three rubber bands holding all the info inside, and dig in.

I've just begun reading the detectives notes when a buzz sounds from the tablet. On screen, I see JJ and Matt coming in the back door, both carrying boxes—Matt with pizza, JJ with a cardboard file box. More cold cases?

My body flushes at the sight of him. Certain parts tingle and I curse silently under my breath. One hand flies to my hair to make sure it's still held back in the band I put it in this morning, and I curse again. Since when do I check my looks before coming face-to-face with JJ?

Get a grip.

I pretend to be deep into the case in front of me when they enter the conference room.

"Lunch time," Matt announces, plunking the pizza boxes on the table.

I barely glance up, trying not to look at JJ and failing miserably. He's wearing a fresh suit, his cheeks clean shaven, and everything about him is perfect as usual. No one would know he was up all night with me.

Unless they saw the smirk he sends me as he lowers his box to the floor next to my chair.

I jerk my gaze from his face and return to studying the notes in my hands, although I can't make sense of any of it with him so close. That cologne of power and safety washes over me.

"I picked up the rest of the cases to review," he says, stalling to look over my shoulder.

I come out of the chair so fast I nearly smack his chin with my head. I drop the papers then scramble to gather them up. Dammit. "Just leave them," I say. "We'll work on them and you...should go."

I feel Matt's eyes on me, and I shoot him a quick glare. He shakes his head and chuckles softly. "I'll grab napkins and a drink. I'll holler at Meg too."

Just like that, he disappears. So much for backup. I can't blame him for not wanting to get in the middle of me and JJ, but it's all I can do not to call out, "chicken," to his retreating back.

JJ picks up a fallen paper and hands it to me, then begins unloading the case files from his box onto the table. "I've sent two CSI teams back to the Beltway area to look for more bodies or anything that might help nail this guy. Meanwhile, I've got a dozen more cases to read through. Who knows, maybe we'll find Tonya, or Avery, or whatever the hell her name is."

He starts dividing them into three piles—one for me, a second for him, and a third for Matt. Which means, he's staying.

"You're too busy to sit here and go through these," I tell him. "Matt and I can handle it."

He calmly takes off his jacket and settles into a chair, eyeing me the whole time as if drawing a line in the sand. "I hope you like sausage and mushroom. The other is some weird bean sprout and curry concoction Matt insisted on. Doesn't even have meat."

Meg walks in, carrying paper plates. "It's Thai Tofu pizza. One of my favorites." She flips open the box lid. "Let me get Haley a couple pieces and I'll help with these files."

Welcome back to the land of the living, I want to say, but in reality we're still digging into death and murder, so I let the inappropriate comment slide. I feel my world spinning slightly out-of-control. While I don't like the idea of Meg reading about murder victims, I know she has a good eye for details, and she must be at a stopping point on the skull. She may be my ticket to get JJ to leave, saving me from sitting here and making a fool of myself.

Matt returns as Meg is leaving to deliver Haley's pizza. "Meg's going to help," I pointedly say to JJ. "She can take your pile. Be sure and grab a slice on your way out."

He ignores me. "Sausage and mushroom for me," he says to Matt, and Matt, the collaborator, obliges by putting two pieces on a plate and sliding them down the table. I narrow my eyes at him, letting him know I'm going to kill him slowly and dismember his body.

Always the risk taker, he grins at me.

Turncoat.

Meg returns, JJ hands out files, I stew. An hour later, the food is gone and we're not even halfway through the files.

JJ's phone rings not for the first time, but unlike the previous dozen calls he's sent to voicemail, he answers this one. "What'cha got, Gomez?"

He's silent but his eyes lock with mine. A chill runs through me. "Right," he says a moment later. "Don't move it until I get there."

I'm already out of my chair, my own form of ESP kicking in. It has something to do with his tone, the look in his eyes. "Another body?"

He nods, grabbing his jacket. "I assume you're going with me?"

Hell yes.

Meg stands, "Me too." She's out the door, probably to get her phone and purse.

"You want me to go?" Matt asks.

"No," I say.

"Yes," JJ answers at the same moment.

We stare at each other, another line in the sand. JJ shrugs. "Up to you, Charlie."

Apparently my death glare works on him better than Matt. Matt is giving me pleading puppy-dog eyes, though. The last thing he wants is to be stuck here going through cold files, and he's already wrapped up the three cases I gave him the other day.

"All right, you can come, but only if you promise to help me with these later."

He jumps up. "Absolutely."

We bail on Haley, and somehow I end up riding with JJ. He says nothing about last night and I don't either, but *Magic Man* lyrics continue to float through my brain.

A storm is moving in and the clouds hang low and ominous over the crime scene as we park and walk to the dig. The air is heavy with the coming rain, and thanks to the boiling clouds, it's dark enough the CSIs need floodlights to work. People are gathered behind the yellow crime scene tape to watch the macabre show and we have to push through the crowd. JJ flashes his credentials to the police officer on guard who waves us through without even looking at them. JJ's face is well known to the locals.

The medical examiner stands over what's left of the decomposed body with her arms crossed. She's already placed it in a black bag for transport and appears annoyed she's been told to wait for the US Attorney to clear removing it from the scene.

But then her gaze lands on Meg and softens. She rattles off details as we get close, unzipping the bag to show us what's left of this poor woman's body. "Body is badly decomposed as you can see. Initial evaluation: adult Caucasian female between eighteen and thirty."

The material of her tank top and yoga pants withstood being buried better than she did.

"Cause of death?" JJ asks.

Gentry gives him a look that says he knows better. "No clue until I get her on the table."

"How long has she been dead?"

He gets the same look, this time with a little more fire. "I need to do testing to determine that. Which I could be doing right now if I wasn't waiting on you."

JJ doesn't back down. "Give me an estimate."

The ME sighs. "Is it going to help solve this case any faster if you know here and now?"

She's a spitfire, this one. Meg covers her chuckle with a fake cough. "Don't let him get to you, Dr. Gentry. He's always like this."

JJ gives the good doctor a self-deprecating smile. One that has charmed many into doing what he wants. He leans in closer like he's going to share a secret and lowers his voice. "Sorry, doctor. It's been a long week, and we potentially have a serial on our hands. An estimate is better than nothing for my timeline if I'm going to figure out who the killer is. This woman could've been killed by a man already in prison, or someone who is still running around."

Could be this smile, or the gravity of his voice. Gentry relents. "My best guess is around two years, but don't hold me to that."

Meg is looking over her right shoulder toward the crowd ten feet behind us. In the distance, thunder rumbles. I feel my sister's tension and follow her gaze. The bystanders are three rows deep. Some look up to the sky just as the first fat drops began to fall.

"What is it?" I ask Meg.

Now Matt is looking at the crowd as well.

"Someone is watching us," Meg murmurs.

Everyone is. Matt and I exchange a glance. JJ's words to the doctor ring in my head...*someone who is still running around.* We know there's a killer on the loose. He visited our office yesterday. Did he murder this woman? If so, is he in the crowd watching us?

"Stay here with JJ," I tell Meg. To Matt, "I'll make my way to the left and sweep toward the middle. You take the right and meet me there."

Matt nods and we take off in opposite directions. No one appears to be paying attention as I walk past two crime scene techs and duck under the tape. I lose myself in the crowd, covertly pulling out my phone and videoing those around me. Most are starting to file off due to the rain, but a few are diehards.

As I'm passing two older women, I see a light blue baseball cap. A man has it pulled low over his face, but I see a quick flash of teeth before he whirls away from me and my camera. Smirking.

My instincts roar to life and I gently push past them, starting to run. My heels sink into the soft dirt. Why didn't I change into my hiking shoes?

At the same moment, the sky opens up and rain pours down.

People jostle me and I lose Mr. Ball Cap for a moment. My pulse is pounding as hard as the rain.

He's fast—disappearing into a slew of parked emergency vehicles. I catch sight of Matt and, the moment he sees me, he knows I'm on the hunt. I point toward the cars and he takes off, meeting me near a cruiser.

Through the pouring rain, I huff out, "Male, five-eight or so, wearing a light blue ball cap. Took off running when he saw me filming the crowd."

Together we search the area, my shoes miring in mud and I curse them. The man is nowhere to be seen. After a few minutes, we circle back and find JJ and Meg waiting for us. The coroner's van is pulling out, the CSIs collecting their tools and calling it a day.

JJ's face is as ominous as the storm clouds. "What the hell, Charlie? Why'd you take off?"

"Why do you think?" I'm out of breath and my shoes are ruined. I play back my video, but Ball Cap isn't on it. Damn, damn, damn. Why didn't I think to film the crowd upon arrival? "Killers often revisit the scene."

"I was right," Meg says, her eyes wide.

I nod, a bitter taste in my mouth. "Our killer was here."

13

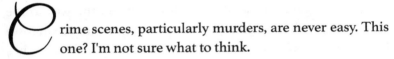rime scenes, particularly murders, are never easy. This one? I'm not sure what to think.

Or feel.

All I know is I'm sitting in Matt's car, a vintage Mustang he restored himself, while pounding rain batters the hood like missiles from the sky. They soaked us while we stood over a decomposed body and I'm now shivering as I wait for the heat to kick in.

In my gut, I know the unearthed woman is another victim of our serial killer. I feel it with every icy stab to my system. Infuriating. All of it. I curl my fingers and as short as my nails are, they dig into my palm, pinching my skin. The pressure refocuses me, forces me to get control of my emotions. Anger won't help now. Calm, rational thought will.

From the corner of my eye, I see Matt glance at me. "What are you thinking, Meg?"

I'm too quiet. He knows that's never a good thing. "She's one of his," I say. "And I'm pissed. We have to stop him."

"I know. But who is he?"

That's the problem. I need to know, and I don't. Not yet, anyway.

"It has to be the same guy who killed Avery. And maybe Emily."

"I'd like to agree, but we don't have enough to go on yet. Don't get ahead of yourself."

Matt's an investigator. He needs all his pieces, his physical evidence, to fit in a nice convenient sequence that tells a story. A book unfolding in front of him. Me? I'm an artist. I rely on cognitive instincts.

Like the ones telling me college-aged blondes in D.C. shouldn't walk alone at night.

Or maybe I'm tired.

Quiet fills the car as Matt battles traffic on the way to the office. As much as I'd like to discuss this case, about what we have—and don't—I can't. The emotional onslaught has drained my energy bucket. I'm smart enough to know I shouldn't battle it. I should allow myself to go home, to crawl into my bed with a mug of herbal tea and watch Full House reruns.

Yet, here I am, refusing to give in to the exhaustion that holds me hostage.

Rather than drive around the building, Matt pulls to the curb in front and I yank the door lever. The low rumble of the Mustang's engine goes silent and I turn back to him.

"I'm coming in with you."

"Why?"

"Because it's dark and a psycho creeped around here yesterday."

My protector. Good for him. As much as it pains me, I smile. "You're a good man."

"I like to think so."

Even still, I need to be alone right now and let my emotions come unglued. "Go home. Taylor is waiting for you and I have a lot of work to do. You can't stay with me all night."

"I won't stay all night. Neither will you."

He's stubborn. I know this about him. In turn, he knows me well enough to figure out we'll get inside, I'll feel guilty from him sitting with me and after an hour we'll both go home.

No one will ever accuse Matt of stupidity.

"I know what you're doing," I inform him.

"Good. Then maybe we won't be here all fucking night."

At that I laugh. "An hour," I say. "Then we'll both go home and sleep."

Thankfully, the rain has slowed to a drizzle as we head to the door. Our jackets are drenched and I'm more than ready to wrap myself in one of the cozy sweatshirts I keep in my office. Matt's phone dings an incoming text and he pauses to check the screen. "I gotta respond to this. Be right in."

Security lights illuminate the front, but I'm more interested in the glow of our interior lamps seeping through the blinds of the window. Haley must still be here. Working late. Even our admin has too much to do.

For her sake, I hope she's locked up. I check the handle and it doesn't budge. Good. As I insert my key, cold wind whips my hair against my face. I tip my head back and inhale fresh air, thankful for each breath. Unlike Emily, Avery, and the woman discovered hours earlier, I'm alive, doing what I love—no matter how emotionally draining—and I'm grateful.

Even if it wrecks me, drives me to a debilitating madness that'll never fully leave me, I'm making a difference. I know I am.

I lift my head, stare at the solid walnut door Charlie insisted on and exhaustion presses down on me like a baby elephant.

Damn, I'm tired. But...Avery. We need to identify her and send her home. Wherever that might be.

I turn the key and the clunk echoes in my head, its energy

shooting straight down my spine. I don't want to be here. My mind keeps telling me that, but my heart can't let go. It wants to work on Avery, so I push open the door.

The desk is empty. More than likely, she's in the powder room or maybe the kitchen area.

"Haley?"

The heels on Matt's worn biker boots clop-clop against the pavement as he strides behind me. "What's up?"

After yesterday's incident a fresh batch of paranoia shreds my already taxed nerves. "She's not answering."

Then I'm in motion, my mind pounding at me to stay put, but my body needs to move. Matt is hot on my heels as I charge the hallway, checking each office.

"Haley?"

"Haley!"

Matt's louder voice echoes mine, but still no answer. I scan my office, frustration mounting. When I step back into the hall, Matt appears in the conference room doorway shaking his head.

"Nothing."

I peer at the back door and...hold on.

Half an inch of the interior edge is visible. It's been pulled closed, but not completely.

"Crap," Matt says, obviously noting the same.

He angles around me and in a few long strides is ripping it open.

No.

That's my first thought. How twisted am I that my only reaction is he's touched the door and obliterated fresh prints?

Morbid. I know.

Outside, he hooks a sharp left half-jogging toward Haley's compact. I go the other way. Why, I'm not sure, but something pulls me, yanks me to the side where a narrow path separates us from the neighboring building.

On my third step I spot the broken streetlight. The one that's supposed to illuminate the corner of the lot and my chest locks up, reminding me to breathe or I'll wind up in a face plant.

Shit.

"Matt!"

A muffled sound bursts from the alley and I halt. Fifteen feet in front of me, shadows move. Two bodies, apparently in a struggle.

"Matt!"

Panic roars at me, filling my ears with a whoosh that doubles my vision. I should stop. I know I should, but something is wrong.

Really wrong.

"Haley!"

I charge toward them, the garbled sounds coming at me again. Closer this time. Something white flashes followed by the clickety-clack of high heels against pavement. Then a scream. A loud piercing one that wreaks of desperation.

My eyes adjust to the blackness and the white—a shirt—comes closer. Suddenly, Haley is there, bearing down on me, her mouth wide as her screams continue to shatter the cool night air.

Before I can say anything, I'm blown sideways, shoved so hard by Matt I'm off my feet and tumbling. I land hard on my hip —*ooff*—and pain rockets down my leg.

Haley is still screaming, her feet barely touching ground as she cuts the corner of the building too close and bumps it. She trips and lands hard on all fours. I jump up and plant myself in front of her, squatting to make eye contact. So she can see it's me.

So she can see she's safe.

The light above the back door reveals wild, unfocused eyes bouncing all over while her wails damn near split my skull. "Haley! It's me. Meg."

Long seconds pass. Five maybe ten. I'm not sure. All I know is her mouth abruptly slams shut and she peers at me with an intensity that drills right through me.

My God. What happened to her?

As if reading my mind, she sits back on her haunches and lifts her head, exposing her neck to me. Blood oozes from a jagged gash that mars her creamy white skin.

"Oh, my God." I drop to my knees and reach for her, bringing her into my arms and squeezing. "You're safe now. I promise. Ssshhh. I'll take care of you."

We stay there, the two of us breathing hard as I look over her shoulder, watching that damn alley where Matt took off running, obviously chasing Haley's assailant.

My mind races with questions. Who was he? Our killer? Did she see him? Why was she in the alley?

All of it will be answered soon enough.

I hope.

Right now, all I hear are Haley's harsh breaths and I pray the shock hasn't blocked her from remembering what happened.

"You're all right," I reassure her, but even I only half believe it. She may never be all right after this. "We should go inside. Lock ourselves in. I'll look at your neck, but we should get you to a hospital."

And call the police.

And Charlie.

And JJ.

So many things to do and I begin to shiver. The shelter of a juicy adrenaline burst is subsiding, replaced with that same consuming rage from earlier.

Inside. We need to get to safety. If her attacker managed to elude Matt, he could come back to finish what he started.

And I'll be goddamned if I'll let him. I have an entire arsenal of weapons on my work table that'll assist me in carving this guy up.

"Cccc...ops," she says.

The police. She wants the police. I let go of her and dig my cell out of my back pocket. "I'll call them. Right now."

I dial 911 and give the operator what information I have.

I pocket my phone again, help Haley to her feet, and walk her inside, my gaze constantly skimming the area. In the distance, a siren sounds. Not too far. Good.

I lock us in and lead Haley to one of the chairs in the kitchen area. Blood runs down her chest, drenching the collar of her blouse. I should be sickened. Part of me is, but it's more about our assistant being attacked than anything else.

The blood? It's almost invisible to me, reminding me violence has become mundane to my sister and me.

Haley tilts her chin up to give me a better view of her wound. It's a two inch gash starting under her left earlobe.

Whatever happened to her, Matt and I got there just in time.

14

CHARLIE

I hate the reek of hospitals even worse than the smell of prison. Can't tell you exactly why, except it has something to do with being at someone else's mercy, not feeling in control.

Internally, I'm shaking from head to toe with anger—at least that's what I tell myself. I have no room for fear, not now, even though the bitter burn of it underneath is what's charging me up.

Haley didn't want to come, but I made her. She was so freaked out, we could barely get her through the interview with the cops. Meg was mothering her, trying to coax her into having a doctor check her, and my nerves were burning with the need to do something. I put my foot down and dragged the poor girl here.

The doctor confirms Haley needs stitches. I hate to be petty, but there's a part of me that feels a bit self-righteous that I made her come. Even if I do loathe hospitals and would've rejected the idea if it had been me in her place.

It's a good thing she's bleeding, in all honesty, because otherwise my fear and anger would rise up to blast her for going into the alley alone. Did I not just spend an hour-plus the other day grilling her about safety and security procedures?

Yeah, sometimes I'm a bitch, but when you're trying to protect people, and they don't follow the rules you've given them, well, if you're me, you get a little bitchy. It's only because I feel the need to protect everyone who works for us. Haley's safety is just as important to me as Meg or Matt's.

"I can take her home," Matt offers. "If you want to get back to the office."

Meg is downstairs looking for vending machines, even though none of us are hungry. I'm pacing the hallway, the stink of alcohol and the sharp tinge of guilt filling my nostrils. We're all dealing with concern in our own ways, and Meg already yelled at me for being a bitch. She probably figured it was better to take her anger and fear to another floor temporarily before we get into a row. "Not necessary. I'll drive her home."

Thank God Matt was there. I can only imagine what might've happened if it had been only Meg. My sister is beyond tough; I have no doubt she can handle herself in a fight. She's taken multiple self-defense courses that I make her review with me on an annual basis. But if the bastard was holding a knife to Haley and threatening her, it wouldn't matter how tough or well-versed in self-defense Meg might be. She would've blamed herself for anything that happened, and she doesn't need that kind of guilt.

JJ strides around the corner just as Matt says, "Goddamn, I should have nailed the asshole. I tried. He's playing with us, and I, for one, am sick of it."

I share his frustration, but I'm relieved Matt didn't end up needing stitches too. Or worse.

After Haley gave her report, JJ left to speak to the chief of police. Even now, there are unmarked cars in strategic places near our office, the duplex I share with my sister, and Haley's apartment, just in case the bastard shows up there, because of

JJ's insistence. When she went out the back to grab files from her car she'd taken home and forgotten to bring in earlier, she interrupted the bastard going through her glovebox. I have no doubt he now knows who she is and where she lives. When she's done receiving stitches, she'll be staying for a few days with a friend across town.

"You did good grabbing the bastard's hat," I say to Matt.

"We got lucky, Charlie. It fell off when he bolted."

"It doesn't matter. You still saw it in the dark."

JJ sent it to the lab with a rush order. We may be able to retrieve DNA and see if it matches any already in the criminal system. On TV and in the movies, they make it sound like every criminal's is on record when in reality, the database is fairly small. So, it's a long shot, but one worth taking.

I look at JJ. "Did you get permission for me to go back to the prison?"

He nods. "You really think Wilson will know who our copycat is?"

"It's possible. Hell, Mickey may have trained him."

The body dug up today can't be Mickey Wilson's work. It's too fresh. But I have a sneaky suspicion he won't like the fact someone took up where he left off. Unless he has a protégé who's feeding him the details after each kill.

At the prison, Mickey tried to take credit for Emily, but I saw right through him. Of course, he called her Tonya, but maybe this Tonya was actually a victim of Mickey's protégé.

I need to question him again, make him feel inadequate, or maybe play on that big, fat ego of his once more and get him to admit someone was helping when he made all those kills. One way or the other, I have to get into his head, get more info. Even if he didn't train this copycat, he might have an idea who it is.

Matt leans on the wall, unconvinced. "We still don't know the guy from the office is the same one who killed these girls."

He's right, but I argue anyway. It's hard to leave bitch-mode once I'm in full steam. "Of course, it is, Matt. The blond wig he left on Meg's skull? And it shows up *the same day* we questioned Mickey? Come on. You know your gut's saying the same thing mine is. Whoever this guy is, he has all the markings of a serial killer, and dollars to donuts, he's the one who's been leaving bodies along the Beltway since Mickey went to prison."

Matt puts his hands in the air in a show of supplication. "I hear you, Charlie. But part of my job is playing devil's advocate. What if we're dealing with two different people?"

I don't want to consider that, because that means I have absolutely no leads on Cap Guy if the DNA doesn't match.

JJ rocks on his heels and crosses his arms. "He's right. We need to look at all the angles."

Perfect. Two against one. I'm only agitated because I know they're right. I pace past the window, biting my bottom lip so I don't start yelling. How long does it take to put in a few stitches? "I want to go to the prison tonight."

"Best I could do is tomorrow morning," JJ says.

I whirl on him. "I'll drive myself. Tonight."

He stays calm in the face of my anger. "They won't let you in. They won't even let *me* in."

What? "You're a U.S. Attorney! You can get in anytime you want. You're not trying hard enough."

He doesn't sigh out loud, but I feel the contained exasperation like a pulsing anger between us. "It's been a long day so I'm gonna let you slide on that. We have to handle this carefully, Charlize, and you know it. Going to see Wilson once without his lawyer present, we got away with. In fact, we're lucky he didn't ask for them. A second time? He's not stupid. He'll either lawyer up or start claiming harassment. He's not directly involved in an open investigation—he lied about Tonya—and the cold cases do not have concrete evidence linked to him, as Matt pointed out, to justify questioning him again without his lawyer present. Which isn't happening under any circumstances until tomorrow."

I bite my lip again and turn away, purposely breathing out through my nose. Control. *Stay in control.*

JJ is right. Matt is too. I have to rein in my chaotic feelings and rely on my cool, levelheaded training.

Another breath.

Mickey will eat up all this attention. It's not like he gets many visitors, and now, a second from us, and this one requires his lawyer?

Visitors... Something in me, a thread, pulls taut.

My head snaps up. Once again I turn to JJ, just as Meg is coming around the corner, her hands full of snacks.

"What did Mickey say?" I roll my hand, trying to tease it out of my brain. "The day we were there? Something about a visitor?"

"He said it was his lucky day," Meg chimes in as if she's been part of our conversation the whole time. "That we were the second visitor he'd had that day."

I snap my fingers. "We need the log from Tuesday," I say to JJ. *Please don't let it be his lawyer,* I think to myself. "We need to know who came to see him before we did."

JJ takes out his phone. "That I can do."

Haley and the doctor emerge from the exam room, Haley looking pale but no longer shaking. Probably because the anti-anxiety pills they gave her kicked in, and I have the feeling she's going to need more of them as she processes the fact she was attacked and nearly had her throat slit by our killer.

Meg shoves the snacks at Matt and reaches for Haley, grabbing her hand and pulling her close as the doctor reels off instructions. After he's done and walking away, she turns to me. "Why?" she asks about the log. "What are you thinking about the other visitor?"

It's just a hunch. I have no reason to believe Mickey's visitor could actually lead us to the man playing with us, teasing us, believing he's smarter than we are. But in this way, he is much like Mickey. While there's no solid proof—the kind Matt needs —my instincts tell me the two men have worked together. They at least know each other.

I don't want to get everyone's hopes up, but you better believe no matter who it is, I am going to be in front of Mickey first thing come morning. Serial killers have a unique psychology. Most are loners, but some work in pairs.

"Charlie?" Meg brings me back. She knows the answer to the question before she asks it. "You think this bastard is a friend of Mickey Wilson's?"

I take Haley's other hand and lead everyone down the hall. "I think our killer's identity has been in front of me this whole time and I was too damn dense to see it."

"*D*evante Bales."

I pause while reading the file Charlie handed me before I walked out of our office and hopped into Matt's Mustang. It's a beautiful morning and on the other side of the roadway the spring sunshine glistens off dewy trees. After this road trip, I might need some time outside, in the woods not far from our office. It's impossible to be sad in the woods. At least I think so. There's something about the earthy smells and fresh air that clears my mind. I suppose that's why I enjoy sitting by the Silver Tail. But there's no time for that today so this will have to do.

"Devante Bales?" Matt muses. "Never heard of him. What's his story?"

I look back at Charlie's insanely organized and typed notes. Me? I'd do it by hand and have comments in all the margins.

"He's a PhD student at American University. Twenty-four years old. Father is a doctor, mother a college professor."

"How do we know this?"

I eye Matt with my foolish-boy look. By now, he's worked with us long enough to know my sister has amazing contacts.

Hackers, FBI and CIA agents, judges. You name it, Charlie knows someone in the field. She's built a career on her connections and knows exactly how to leverage them.

Chances are the information we have on Devante Bales is courtesy of Teeg, hacker extraordinaire, at the Justice Team.

"Right," Matt says. "PhD? What subject?"

I check my notes again. "Justice, Law & Criminology. School of Public Affairs."

Being a former cop, one with a bachelor's in Criminal Justice, Matt understands the lure of studying criminal behavior.

"So, he's in a grad program in D.C.. Let's assume he wants to be a federal agent."

"Or a lawmaker."

"Politics?" Matt mulls that over for a few seconds, rolling his bottom lip out before offering a solid nod. "Yeah. I'll buy that."

"If we find him, we can ask. Along with why he visited Mickey Wilson right before us the other day."

I flip to the driver's license photo of Devante, a clean-cut biracial man with round glasses that give him a studious look. His hazel eyes, more green than brown, capture my attention. This kid's face belongs on a magazine cover. It might be The Economist versus GQ, but this was a fine looking man.

And, God knew, plenty of serial killers had been handsome. Gorgeous even. Those looks helped lure innocent women to places they had no business going.

At best, Devante is studying serial killers.

At worst, he *is* a serial killer.

A copycat gleaning information from Mickey, who excels at every characteristic of the most loathsome humans.

"Let's hope he's doing research," Matt says, apparently reading my mind.

We spend the rest of the ride in silence and I close my eyes. There's no headrest in the vintage car, but I do my best to slouch and tip my head back. I need to meditate for a few minutes and get my mind right. In general, I'm not built for investigative work. It drains my energy. But I can't look at Emily every day and do nothing when this case might have something to do with her.

I owe it to her.

And Avery.

Matt pulls into a parking garage down the street from the address on the copy of the license. According to his schedule, another gift I'm assuming came from Teeg, Devante works in the tutoring center on campus on Saturdays at eleven until three. It's barely nine-thirty. We've timed this well.

We park and walk the block to the apartment. There's a buzzer at the outer door and a speaker about to fall out of its enclosure. Matt shoves the piece back into place, only to have it stubbornly pop out again. Hopefully, it's not a sign of how this meeting will go.

His mouth tips down at the corners and just as I think he's about to press the buzzer, he looks at me. "How do you want to do this?"

"Let's skip good cop, bad cop. At least at first. If he's not cooperative, I'll be the former. You can play the understanding male, rolling your eyes at me and earning his trust. That work?"

He shrugs and pokes the buzzer. "Sure."

"Hello?" A groggy and deep male voice calls from the speaker.

"Yeah, hey, Devante," Matt says, all cool and casual. "I'm Matt Stevens. An investigator working a murder case involving Mickey Wilson. I know you saw him the other day. I could use your help. Got a sec?"

The speaker goes silent, but this is D.C. and a blaring car horn won't be denied its moment to make my ears bleed. I whirl around to give the driver a nasty glare and find two cars at a standstill due to a double-parked cab.

This is why I don't live in the city. Too much noise and drama.

"Idiot," Matt mutters.

A loud *zzzppp-zzzppp* followed by the thunk of the disengaging door lock spurts adrenaline into my bloodstream. Devante has granted us access. Here we go...

Once inside, I glance at Matt. "That was easy."

"I kept it casual. Plus, some intellectuals like talking about themselves. I took a shot he might want to brag about his prison visit."

The elevator, one of those old rickety deals with the sliding inner gate, carries us to the fourth floor where we knock on door 410.

Devante opens said door, round glasses in place, his cheeks spotted with fine facial hair that, if given a month, still wouldn't become a beard. His white T-shirt is beyond wrinkled, the basketball shorts not much better. In the two images—driver's license and student ID—I've seen of him, he wore an Oxford shirt, the collar pressed and stiff. His current clothing along with his initial groggy greeting via the buzzer leads me to believe we've woken him up.

"Hi." Matt extends his hand and the two men shake. "I'm Matt Stevens from Schock Investigations. This is Meg Schock. A forensic sculptor."

I nod and extend my hand. Devante's palm is warm, his grip firm but not obnoxious or prolonged. Manners. His parents taught him well.

"A sculptor. That's cool." His gaze shoots to Matt then me. "You're working a case?"

"Yes," I say. "It's a cold case. We believe it's a serial killer."

His mouth opens, forming a perfect O. "Whoa."

He steps back, pulling the door open.

Boom.

We're in.

Intellectuals. Such an interesting group.

The apartment is small and neat with a galley kitchen, breakfast bar and an open area containing a plaid loveseat. A battered coffee table holds a single photography book. A rocking chair completes the seating. Along the wall in the corner is a tall oriental screen. I spot the edge of a blanket peeking out and suspect the screen hides a bed that pulls from the wall.

Studio apartment.

He waves to the loveseat and Matt and I drop into it. The cushion sinks under Matt's heavier weight and my body lists. I don't want to be conducting this interview while getting cozy, so I lean to my right, countering gravity.

Devante takes the chair, sets his phone on the table between us and holds his hands wide.

"How can I help?"

I take the lead. "I understand you visited Mickey Wilson the other day."

"Yes. I'm working on a research paper for my doctorate."

Research paper.

I lift my eyebrows, pretending to be at least partially surprised. "What are you studying?"

The corner of his mouth lifts. "Ms. Schock, I'm gonna guess you know the answer. Why else would you be here?"

Touché.

As much as I don't want to, I like this guy. If he's a serial killer, he's a charming one. Even I, with my hardened senses, recognize his appeal.

From my messenger bag, I retrieve the folder with Charlie's notes, set it on my lap and flip it open. "Okay. Since you've busted me, we'll get right to it. We're working a cold case. Two in fact. Mickey has claimed responsibility for both murders, but we have doubts. We're hoping you might be able to tell us something regarding these cases." I roll one hand. "Since you're working on a research paper with a serial killer. Maybe he's shared things with you."

Devante rises and moves to a rectangular dining table against the wall. Beside it are three plastic stackable drawers with a printer on top. The table, probably a hand-me-down or a garage sale find given the nicks on the legs, is doubling as a desk.

"I'm happy to help in any way," he says. "I have my notes from my meetings with Mickey right here."

Meetings. As in plural.

Matt slides me a sideways glance. "So, you've been there before?"

"Oh sure. Four, maybe five times. He's a total head case."

That's one way to put it.

"What exactly is this paper you're working on?"

He shuffles through a perfect stack of manila folders, reading the tabs of each before pulling one out and facing us again. "I'm comparing common characteristics of male versus female serial killers. I've interviewed five men and three women so far."

He walks back and holds a file out. "It's rather fascinating."

Just like that. *Here you go. Read all you like about the psycho I'm studying.*

A chill lances down my arms. How could this topic be so casual to all of us? What have we become that this level of violence doesn't shock or intimidate us?

It's something I can't think too hard about, so I open the folder and skim the first page. A handwritten summary of a conversation with Mickey. Devante's penmanship is excellent. The words contain neat block letters—all caps—that form freakishly perfect square paragraphs.

Matt peers over my shoulder. "What have you determined so far?"

"The most common is males choose strangers as their victims while females tend to kill people they know."

"I see. And Mickey?"

"Strangers. Every time. Blondes. And he slits their throats. It makes him, er, he gets sexual gratification from it."

Lord.

"Has he told you about any of his victims? Where he's buried them? How many?"

"No. Nothing like that. We don't talk specifics. It's mostly about his upbringing and such. He's highly intelligent. He says his IQ is one forty-five, but I can't confirm."

Interesting. I'm sure my sister already knows this since she studied Mickey in great detail before his trial. "A genius."

"According to him. No proof though. I'm not sure how much you know about him, but his mother forced him to sleep in a locked basement. She was a single mom trying to find a husband. When the men saw him, they'd leave her." Devante shrugs. "They didn't want a woman with children."

Matt shakes his head, lets out a grunt. "So she locked him in when men came over."

"Yes. She hid him. Told him no one could ever love him." He waggles a finger at his file. "You'll see it in my notes. I believe slashing his victim's throats is symbolic of shutting his mother up."

Well, nearly decapitating someone would be one way to do it. "Did she ever remarry?"

"She did. She found a man with children of his own. By then, Mickey was severely damaged."

This is also in Charlie's notes, confirming my sister's research before the bastard's trial. "I see."

Devante leans forward, rests his elbows on his knees and lets out a long sigh. "Look, he's a messed up dude. He belongs in prison."

Something in his tone forces me to set his notes down and focus on him. "But?"

He shrugs. "I can see why his victims became his victims. He connects with people. Maybe he stopped to talk to them, and they figured he was harmless. I don't know."

Maybe he asked them to show him their boobs. "Do you plan on visiting him again?"

"It depends. If I need more info, he's always willing to talk."

Devante reaches for the coffee table and taps his phone screen. "Oh, wow. It's getting late. I have to be at work in an hour."

He stands but I remain seated. I'm not done yet. I want copies of his notes. Up to this point he's been cooperative. Almost too much so. That might be my own suspicions bubbling up, but when it comes to this case, I can't be too trustful of anything.

Or anyone.

I tap the folder still in my lap. "Do you mind if I take copies of what's in this folder?"

He blinks once. Then again. And again.

Apparently I've confused him. Then it hits me. This guy has been visiting serial killers and suddenly two investigators show up at his door. He's not stupid. He knows he's either a suspect or I want his research.

But there's something else. His relaxed body language. It disturbs me, but my brain won't latch on to specifics. It swirls in my head like a fog that I can't grab.

"You want...copies? Of my research?"

I hold up my hand. "For reference. I promise I won't share it with anyone outside of our firm, which includes my sister, Charlie." I point to Matt. "And Matt. Who's already heard it all."

"What are you going to do with it?"

"Study it. I have two skulls, reconstructions of murdered

young women, in my office. I want to bring them justice." I hold up the folder. "I believe your notes can help."

I peer up at him, waiting for him to decide and the fog in my head clears, makes room for a new idea.

"In fact," I say, "if you'd like to visit my office and see what we're all about, you're more than welcome."

This seems to perk him up. "I could make it part of my research. Include it in my paper."

"Why not? My sister is a forensic psychologist. A profiler. She worked Mickey's case in the past. I'm sure she'd be willing to do an interview."

"Oh, man. That'd be awesome."

Awesome, indeed.

I spend the next five minutes snapping cell phone pictures of his notes. When I finish, I hand the folder back to Devante, and Matt and I make our way to the street where morning sunshine warms my cheeks. I take three full breaths, let all the fresh oxygen invade my body.

"Visit the office?" Matt says. "What the hell was that about?"

"I want to get him on video. Coming in the back door."

"Why?"

"To see if he looks like the guy in the wig."

16

CHARLIE

*M*ickey has refused to speak to us, his attorney letting me know in no uncertain terms that "Mr. Wilson has nothing further to say." I sat around this morning waiting for the go-ahead, and instead wasted my time, while my sister and Matt do the legwork of digging into Devante Bales.

JJ is putting pressure on whoever he can, but our convicted serial killer has decided he's the star of the show. Like a king on his throne, he'll let us know when he's ready to talk, if ever. Meanwhile, he's been spilling his guts to this PhD student with regularity.

From what Matt and Meg told me after their visit, Devante doesn't fit a stereotypical serial killer. None of us are completely ruling him out yet, but on the surface, he seems like a normal twenty-four-year-old college kid. I've got Teeg running a background check and should have it by the time I return to the office.

Devante is due to visit us after his three-o'clock class. Heads-up thinking by my sister to get him in our environment where we can put a little pressure on him and see what result we get. Meg and I scanned his interview notes while we ate a quick lunch, but I had to bail in order to deliver a DNA kit to Yvonne after not being able to yesterday.

I arrive at her house the same time Juanita pulls in. Her smile is warm, but doesn't quite meet her eyes as we exchange hellos on the way to the front door. It's only been a few days since she visited the office, but I swear she's lost weight. She has another colorful scarf covering her head, but her skin has taken on a pallor that makes me want to rush her to the hospital.

The clock is ticking. On her, on me.

It's going to come down to Yvonne's mitochondrial DNA to prove—or disprove—this family connection.

Half an hour later, I leave the two women chatting as if they are indeed mother and daughter. If nothing else, they've formed a bond that can help Juanita as she faces the coming weeks. A part of me worries their DNAs will not match, and we won't have time to find Juanita's true biological parents before she passes.

I call my dad and a sense of peace washes over me hearing his voice. I'm one of the lucky ones to have parents who love and support me every step of the way, and I can't imagine being at the end, only to find out I might die without knowing who gave me life.

"If you're calling to tell me about the serial killer, Charlize"—Dad never says hello, just jumps right in as if we've been having a conversation all along—"I already saw it on the news."

"Hi, Dad," I say pointedly. "I'm good, how are you?"

He snorts at my reminder to have manners, and I laugh. "Actually, I'm calling about the woman I mentioned earlier this week. Juanita. I have DNA matches I'd like you to look into, see who they turn up and contact the most likely candidates to help us figure out her parentage."

Dad's been retired from the Army for nearly fifteen years. He was career military, and he's the one I've gotten many of my traits from, from my slender build to my need for organization and rules.

"Done." He's worked other cases like this with me and needs no further instructions. "Send them to me and I'll start right away."

"I'll have Haley"—I stop, remembering she's not in the office and for good reason. I should probably check on her this afternoon, at least send a text and see how she's doing. Meg probably already has. "I'll email them to you."

"Now, what about this serial killer?"

I have a lot of work to do this afternoon and evening but seeing my dad might help me feel less agitated and angry. "Can you come over for dinner? I don't have time to make anything, but I can order pizza. I'll show you all the files and my notes."

"Cripes. Your mom is dragging me to some fundraising event tonight. She's insisting I wear my uniform. Can you believe it?"

Of course, I can. Though he complains, Dad loves to dress up with all of his medals and bars. "Wear it and have a good time. Kiss mom for me."

I drop off Yvonne's kit and get to the office before Devante is due. Someone has started a fresh pot of coffee, the scent pleasantly filling my nose as I enter the back door. Normal, that's what it feels like.

Music is coming from Meg's work area. Matt is in the conference room having cleared the table. He brought in the landline from Haley's desk and is fielding calls. I give him a wave in greeting as I pass, and he calls out, "They're on your credenza."

Meaning the files. I'll have to haul them home tonight to start going through them again. I plop into my chair, tuck my purse away, and glance at the background check I requested.

At three o'clock, I'm sitting on the edge of Haley's desk, waiting for our guest to arrive. The seconds tick by on the wall clock. I still haven't purchased a new battery for my watch and Meg's is around my wrist. I tinker with it as the second hand on the wall passes the twelve again.

Yeah, I'm a stickler for being on time. This guy is a college student, but he's no freshman. I doubt his professors put up with him being late.

At three-o-five, Meg enters with her favorite coffee mug in hand, giving me a raised brow. I shake my head. No Devante. She goes to the window and stares at the parking lot. Knowing her, she is mentally willing him to show up.

At quarter after, Matt stumbles in, handing me a couple of pink message slips. None need an immediate return call and I lay them on the desk.

"No sign of our guy?" he asks.

"Nope." I swing my legs, my heels thudding against the wood of the desk, irritation in each strike.

Meg sends me a curt glance. "Maybe he got stuck in traffic."

Or he's guilty of something.

I'm thinking back to what Matt and JJ said about exploring other options. "Matt?"

"Yeah?"

"Text Haley and ask if she knows Devante. Send her a picture in case she knows him by another name."

"Haley?" Meg's frown deepens. "Why would she know him?"

"She probably doesn't, but there's a possibility she has a stalker." It's an angle I should've looked at before. Both times our boy showed up, it was when Haley was here alone. "I want to rule out that our visitor isn't simply a stalker who has nothing to do with Mickey Wilson or the cold cases we're investigating."

Matt nods and points at me as he heads back to the conference room. "Smart."

Once he's gone, Meg looks outside again. "You don't really believe she has a stalker."

"Like I said, we need to rule it out. Devante's her age and she hangs around a lot at the college bars. They could've crossed paths at one time or another. He may be guilty of stalking but not killing anyone."

An audible sigh from Meg. "What do we do if he doesn't show?"

"His background check is clear, no priors or anything outside parking tickets. I'll dig deeper and go through his college history and social media tonight."

"I'll come over and help."

That evening, however, it's JJ who shows up on my doorstep, sushi and a fresh bottle of wine in hand.

"I can't..." I start, tongue-tied when I see him looking so absolutely delicious and memories of the prior night flash through my tired brain. "You can't be here."

"Meg said you're working like usual." He shoots me an evil grin. "I'm taking care of you whether you like or not, Schock."

He barges in, gently shoving me out of the way.

I'm ashamed to say I don't protest nor throw him out, but the stacks of files on missing girls and Devante's interview notes sitting on my dining room table feel like a black hole waiting to suck me in. Having help to make the evening a little less horrific is welcome.

Of course, tomorrow I'll give my sister grief. She sent JJ instead of showing up herself.

We eat, drink, and pour over details until midnight. I keep going back to Devante's notes, Mickey talking about his mother, how awful she was to him whenever she had a boyfriend around. I read over a section about the man she ended up with, his kids. I remember most of it from my pretrial evaluation of Mickey, but it's good to get a fresh perspective.

Connections. It's all about them, the threads that weave people together. Families especially, but also coworkers, the people in your neighborhood, at your church or synagogue, even the clerk who checks your groceries. Everyone knows a piece about you or may share your secrets. They help put random pieces of any puzzle into a whole. It's why I love assisting people with tracing their ancestry, uncovering buried secrets, finding those oh-so-important connections.

I didn't hang around for Mickey's trial after I pronounced him fit for it. I need to get my hands on the transcripts. In Devante's notes, Mickey claims his stepsiblings hated him, especially the girls. Apparently, Mickey used their dolls to practice terrible things on.

Devante's earliest interviews include Mickey laughing about how weak and whiny they were. I have a feeling they're lucky he didn't do the same to them as he did their dolls.

JJ and I move to my sofa after a bit, my feet in his lap. His suit coat is off, and his button-down shirt is open at the collar. He squeezes one of my toes when he sees me chewing on my bottom lip. "What is it?"

My brain keeps circling back to Mickey's stepfamily. His mother. "I need the transcripts from Mickey's trial." If I were still in law enforcement, I could get them myself, and these days, I might ask Teeg to hack into the appropriate department and retrieve them for me. But with my own personal DA at my disposal, it's better to use him. More legal and less likely to get me into hot water. "Due to the graphic details regarding the victims, the judge sealed chunks of them so the press couldn't print the gory particulars."

JJ just looks at me, playing dumb.

I nudge him with my foot. "Can you get them for me?"

"Maybe."

I kick him. Not hard, but enough. "Why *maybe*?"

"Quid pro quo." He gives me a wolfish grin. "What are you going to do for me?"

"Shoot you in the ass, if you keep it up."

His deep laughter jiggles the couch and soon I'm joining in. There's no real reason for it, but we've both been so tense and stressed out, it feels good to let loose. Once more, I'm reminded of what this man does to me.

Feeds me. Makes me laugh. Helps me solve cases.

He reaches for my hand, his eyes sparking with that predatory look. "I'll get you the transcripts. What's your take on this Devante kid?"

He never showed and didn't respond to Matt's calls or messages. Haley insists she doesn't know him. He's probably a normal college kid, but... "I just don't know."

17

MEG

*a*t seven a.m. there's a soft knock on my front door. A quick *tap-tap-tap* that's been my sister's calling card from the day we moved in here. Since I'm a creature of habit, she knows I've just finished my morning meditation. I'm a firm believer my mood will set the tone of the day and doing it right after my shower keeps my energy balanced. Something I desperately needed after Devante blew us off yesterday.

As a result, I went to bed aggravated and spent most of the night berating myself.

Fatigue has settled on me, pressing in and shooting a variety of aches straight down my legs as I move toward the door.

I refuse to let that rotten energy take over. As dog-tired as I am, as heavy as I feel, there's important work to be done and it needs a positive attitude.

I set my phone and earbuds on the entry table I found at a flea market. I tend not to buy used furniture—God only knows what kind of weirdness it might carry. A friend likes to boast she won Al Capone's desk at an auction years back and now keeps it in her bedroom.

Al Capone's desk.

In her bedroom.

Talk about crazy. No way in hell I'm bringing that into my house. He could've carved up a body on that thing.

My table though? The expertly carved legs drew me in, and I immediately wanted it. Ten minutes of questioning the merchant and receiving assurances he'd made it the week prior and it hadn't been anywhere but his home, I loaded it into my van. Am I nuts?

Probably.

I can't worry about it.

Charlie knocks again. "Meg?"

"I'm here."

I open the door and my stomach collapses. So much for starting with positive energy. My sister isn't alone. The fact JJ is with her isn't a shock. His car has been parked in our shared driveway at certain times the last few days. Those being late at night and early in the morning.

During those visits, he's been the stealth bomber of lovers. Coming and going in silence and avoiding me seeing him.

"JJ," I say. "No offense, but this can't be good."

"I'm sorry." Charlie gets straight to the point. That's her style and more than likely she's figured out I know this isn't a social call. Not this early with JJ and his wrinkled suit in tow.

I push my shoulders back, readying myself for whatever news they have. As long as it's not our parents, I can deal with it. "What is it?"

Charlie comes inside, waving JJ in behind her. "JJ got a call. We have another body."

Another...body.

A huge rush of air blasts between my lips. It's not quite relief, but it's a whole lot better than where my mind had taken me seconds ago. All I know is my mother and father aren't dead.

For a few seconds, I'm polarized. Just standing there unable to move. Charlie retreats a step, but I put my hands up. Someone has died, more than likely been murdered. What right do I have to receive comfort or coddling?

Finally, I close the door. "I'm fine. Tell me about the body. Is it..." How do I ask this? "...one of ours?"

Meaning is she a young blonde found on or near the Beltway.

Charlie nods. "She was discovered at one-thirty this morning a quarter mile from the Beltway. Some idiot couple riding home from a bar had a fight and the woman threw her husband's phone out the window. He stopped to look for it and stumbled over our victim."

"My God."

"The M.E. said she hasn't been dead twenty-four hours."

Good.

Excellent actually. Twisted, I know. I'm not oblivious to the poor woman being brutally murdered. It's tragic and horrifying and at some point, I'll experience rage over the injustice.

But we have a *body*. With skin and organs and cartilage.

I automatically form questions regarding DNA and blood under the nails. What about semen or saliva on her body? Hair? The killer could've left any number of possible leads.

"Before you ask," Charlie says, "I don't know about trace evidence. I haven't been able to reach anyone at the lab."

"Has she been identified?"

"Not yet," JJ says. "She was wearing a denim skirt and long-sleeved T-shirt. We estimate her age to be late teens-early twenties."

"Same manner of death as the others?"

"Yes."

I don't press him. If she died in the same way, I don't need the nitty-gritty details of a woman being nearly decapitated one day after I interviewed a possible suspect.

Could I have...? Oh, no.

"You don't know it's him," Charlie says.

Devante. That's who we're talking about. We both know it. The kid—man, really, because he's no adolescent studying serial killers and using academia as an excuse. Research, my ass.

I poke my finger at Charlie. "Don't tell me what I don't know. He was a no-show at our office yesterday and hasn't returned any of my calls. We have no idea where he is."

"It doesn't make him a killer," JJ says.

Well, thank you so much, Emperor of Cold Cases. "It doesn't *not* make him one."

JJ concedes the point with a sideways tilt of his head.

Still in my yoga pants and shirt, I angle around my sister and head to my bedroom where I slide into flip flops and grab a brush to run through my hair.

Charlie watches me, knowing full well whatever I'm about to do, she can't stop me. "Slow down, sis."

"I'm going to the morgue."

"It's seven in the morning."

As if that matters? "So? Someone will be there." I point at JJ. "He'll get me in." I open the front door, wave one arm for them to hurry the hell up. "Out."

JJ takes one step but is stopped by Charlie's hand latching onto his forearm. "You're not going there, Meg."

My sister is rarely wrong. Today, she is. Dead wrong.

"I *am*. With or without you. I need to see her."

"Why?"

Why? I open my mouth to enlighten her, to tell her she can shove her lecture straight up her protective ass because I'm done listening. There's a maniac running around killing beautiful young women and we can't find him.

Except...nothing.

The only sound comes from the bushes outside my front

window. A cricket who clearly hasn't realized he should shut up. I stare at the gray, morning sky. Moisture that comes with a whopper of an impending storm surrounds me.

Rain.

Thank God we found her before it hit. I think about her, cold and alone, tossed like garbage on the side of the road. I can't stand it, that vision that invades my mind—her throat carved open, arteries savagely severed, blood everywhere. My arms tremble and I lock my teeth together. *Please, please, please.* I can't fall apart right now. Not in front of Charlie and JJ. What right do I have? Everyone I love is safe.

"Meg, there's nothing—"

I whirl on my sister. "Don't," I say through my gritted teeth. "Don't tell me there's nothing I can do. Someone has to do *something*. It might as well be me. I'm going to the morgue. You can either leave with me or lock up. I really don't care. You're not stopping me though."

"What's the—"

JJ breaks free of Charlie's grasp, gives her hand a squeeze and steps closer to me. "No fighting. We've got shit to do." He leaves, breezing by me in that broad-shouldered, I-will-fix-this way that is so much a part of him. "Let's go, Meg. I'll get you into the morgue. Then we need to find out who this woman is."

I march after him leaving Charlie standing in my foyer. "Who she *was*," I say with plenty of snark, "because some son of a bitch left her butchered."

An hour later, I'm standing over the young woman's body. A sheet covers her to the top of her neck, obviously hiding the damage. Until we identify her, she'll be known as Jane Doe. That alone twists me into fierce knots that damn near double me over. My head is throbbing, my ears buzzing as rage fires in my core and spreads to my limbs.

Devante Bales.

I can't help but think this is his work. It can't be a coincidence that yesterday I poked and prodded at his research, asking questions about Mickey and now we have yet another victim.

"Meg?"

Dr. Gentry's no-nonsense voice interrupts my internal hissy fit. I force my gaze away from the woman on the table and turn toward her. "What do we know?"

She's wearing her usual scrubs and lab coat and the skin under her eyes sags from a lack of sleep. She's no doubt been with this woman's body most of the night.

"Not a lot. We're processing evidence. You shouldn't be here. I'm sure you know that."

I nod. "Thank you for letting me in."

Dr. Gentry folds her arms. "I like you. I'm sure you know that too. And forgive me if I'm being condescending, but I worry about you. You get too emotional. Too attached to the victims."

She's been to this show with me before. Every time we have a cold case, I come looking for her. Picking her brain, begging to see the body. Anything that'll help me with a reconstruction. "Someone has to."

Dr. Gentry lifts one shoulder. "I agree. But you go too far. It's not healthy."

I look back at Jane. Jane *Doe*. I understand the need for the generic identity, but I still despise giving a victim a meaningless name when she's already had her life stolen.

It's disgusting.

To me anyway.

"She has loved-ones somewhere. I need to do something," I choke out the words, pushing them through my dry throat.

"We *are*. We're working on identifying her. One step at a time, Meg. That's all we can do."

She sets her hand on my shoulder and the weight slaps at the rage swirling inside me. Unlike earlier, with my sister and JJ, I allow Dr. Gentry to coddle me.

"Go to your office," she says. "I'll update JJ when we have something. I can't have you here."

I meet her eyes and all I see is warmth. She must be a mother. The realization hits that I don't know this woman at all. Not in the way it counts. Not on a personal level. "Can I—" I inhale, and the sharp, antiseptic odor burns my nostrils. I clear my throat. "Can I have a minute with her? Before I go."

Dr. Gentry sighs. "Ah, Meg. You're hopeless, aren't you?"

I know what she means. We're both aware she could spend hours trying to convince me I get too involved, that I need to put my emotional armor on and not open myself up.

It'll never happen. That's what makes me good at what I do. If it means I'm hopeless, I'll live with it.

"Two minutes," I say. "And I'm out of your way. I promise."

"Two minutes. Then I'm kicking you out. Don't touch her."

"Yes, ma'am."

She shuffles out, her rubber soled shoes squeaking against the tile. The door closes behind her and I look back at Jane. Needing something to do with my hands, I fold my arms. That feels too...cold. Distant. I drop them back to my sides.

The sheet that covers her reveals the ugly, jagged wound that destroyed the long column of her neck. I shift my gaze to her sculpted cheekbones and full lips. In life, she had to have been a stunner. A model maybe.

"I'm sorry."

It sounds lame. Even to me. Still, she deserves to hear it. To know she didn't deserve this. Intellectually, I know her death isn't my fault. Even if Devante Bales is a copycat killer and my questioning him caused a psychotic break. It's his.

I know that.

Yet, looking at this girl, I feel...responsible.

Pressure builds in my knuckles and I look down to where I've clenched my fists too hard. I stretch my fingers, releasing the pressure as I bring my gaze back to Jane. "We'll find him. I promise you, we'll find him."

18

CHARLIE

The local cops are going crazy and have frozen me out for now. The press is equally so, spreading fear among the public about a serial killer.

They're not wrong.

What bothers me more than all of that is the fact my sister has shut me out. It's her coping style, and it works for her, but it drives me batty. Gentry already called to tell me Meg was talking to the dead Jane Doe. I really had no words. I don't find it unusual—a little concerning, yes—but this is how Meg deals, how she processes life and death, violence and injustice.

The psychologist in me knows she's mentally healthier then 99% of the general population. I admire that about her, because I'm pretty sure my methods aren't nearly as healthy, even if they appear normal to the casual observer.

Which is why I'm at my desk, burying my nose in the trial transcripts from Mickey Wilson's case. The police are looking for Devante as a person of interest, and JJ is out making speeches and running the investigation from the U.S. Attorney's office the best he can. As soon as the public gets a whisper of *serial killer*, all hell breaks loose, and I have a feeling I won't see him the rest of the day.

Another reason to bury my head in the transcripts—I don't have to face what's going on between us. Last night, we didn't have sex. A first for us. I fell asleep in his arms on the couch, and in the wee hours of the morning, he carried me into the bedroom and crawled in beside me. We were still sleeping when the call came in about the Jane Doe.

The third thing I don't want to think about is this girl. Yesterday at this time, she had no idea her life was about to end. A young woman with her whole future ahead of her cut short because the killer got itchy.

Premeditated murder is thought out, planned. The single fact the killer dumped the body, as if in a hurry, rather than taking the time to bury her like he did the others, tells me he was acting on sudden impulse. Organized killers use one place and dispose of the body in another, leaving a clean crime scene with little evidence. While the girl fits the parameters of our investigation, our killer appears to have attacked and killed her in the same spot he left her body, suggesting he's under stress and needed a quick release. The most likely reason is because we're on his trail.

I scan the transcripts, stopping here and there to read different people's testimonies. He was of average intelligence, regardless of what he told Devante, fairly social, and held a regular day job.

Like Meg, I want to jump to the conclusion Devante is our new killer. He's college-educated, social, and has copious notes with details about Mickey's kills. Somehow, I just don't see the two of them fitting together, but it doesn't mean he isn't the one who took Jane's life.

Contrary to popular belief, most serial killers stay in a local area. The highly intelligent ones don't keep trophies or souvenirs at their residence, but I sent Matt to Devante's apartment anyway. The cops can't get in without a search warrant; Matt is pretty handy with a lock pick, and I'm determined to stop this killer before he strikes again, even if I have to break the law. I was going to hit Devante's myself, but Matt insisted he would do it. Dumb guy likes to live on the edge, which I totally respect, even admire at times. It takes a lot for me to bypass the law, and he jumps at it every chance he gets.

Poor Taylor. She's got her hands full with him.

My desk phone rings and I ignore it, reading another section. I had Matt transfer all calls to my office since everyone else is gone. The ringing is like the throbbing of my pulse, poking at me, and I glance at the ID screen to see it's the last person on earth I want to talk to right now—Juanita Jones.

The DNA results for her mother should be in, but I've been so caught up with this case since yesterday, I've totally blown them both off. Guilt eats at my stomach and I chew on the inside of my cheek, considering my options.

I can't put her off for long, but there's no point in wasting breath telling her I don't have the results. I pick up my cell phone and call my friend at Family Ties as the landline goes to voicemail. Five minutes later, I have news Juanita doesn't want to hear.

Yvonne is not her mother.

I was afraid of this, pretty much sure of it, in fact. I call my dad. "Any luck with the cousins?"

"Good morning to you too, Charlize." It's almost noon, but he's a stickler for details. "Yes, I have a lead, and I'm meeting with him at four p.m. for coffee. He was a little... surprised, you might say, at the idea of a lost cousin. He's quite the genealogy buff, I guess, and was sure he had located every living relative in his family tree already." I hear him shifting and can imagine him getting comfortable in his big recliner. "Now, tell me about the serial killer."

At least he's got something I can pass to Juanita to soften

the blow of finding out she is once more without her biological parents. I play with my—Meg's—watch as I fill him in on the basic details he hasn't already heard on the news. "Meg is taking this hard, Dad. I'm worried about her."

"Me too, but you can't protect her from everything, Charlize, no matter how badly you want to."

He knows me so well. "She needs to go to her happy place." Dad knows what I'm talking about. Meg has a favorite spot in the woods near our parents' home where she likes to decompress and connect with nature. I decompress by going to the gym and punching things or going to the shooting range and blasting holes into paper targets. My sister sketches flowers and trees while I imagine taking out every bad guy I've ever come across. Which version is more sane? "Could you talk to her and see if she'll visit you for a few days? Tell her mom needs her."

Meg never ignores our mother's requests, just like I never ignore our father's. He makes one now. "Only if you promise to come with her."

A part of me begs to spend the next few days with them, get away from all the stress and pressure of this case, of Juanita's dying wish, of JJ's constant presence. I fiddle with the ring on my finger and tell him a half-lie. "I would love to. If you can get her to say yes, I'll pack my bags and be there with bells on."

We say our goodbyes and I call Juanita. I don't want to dump the new information on her over the phone, but I don't have time to go for coffee with her like my dad would. It goes to voicemail, saving me some of the awkward conversation we need to have. I give her the good news, rather than the bad, letting her know my father is in contact with someone who's directly related to her. Hopefully this person will be open to meeting her and telling her about her biological family.

That done, I refill my cup, hating the eeriness of the too-quiet office and wondering if the serial killer is somewhere outside, watching the building. I go to one of the windows and adjust the blinds to see out. There are plenty of areas nearby where he could be hiding.

Just for spite, I hold up my middle finger, almost hoping, *daring* him to come at me while I'm alone. He likes to use the back, so when I return to my office, I sweat and grunt and shove my desk out into the hallway facing the back exit. My gun is fully loaded, and I flip the safety off, setting it on the desk. I sit back, sipping my coffee. *Come on, you bastard. Come and get me.*

Rain begins to fall outside, and minutes go by. No one pulls into the driveway, no one sneaks by the windows, no one shows up on any of my security cameras. I pick up the transcript and start reading.

I skip to the testimonies given by Mickey's stepsiblings. There were two sisters and a brother. The younger sister, Dixie, provided the majority of testimony, stating her biological brother, Billy Ray, protected her and the older girl, Bonnie. According to her, Mickey tormented them, stole their dolls and did unspeakable things to them. He threatened them, and there were times when they were afraid to go to sleep since he'd vowed on more than one occasion to kill them while they slept.

Nice.

Billy Ray, at the ripe age of thirteen, took on Mickey more than once, the two of them ending up in brawls that scared the sisters. It appears Billy Ray got the crap beat out of him more than once, as evidenced by several emergency room visits presented in court.

When I evaluated Mickey, we talked about his family, but glossed over these bits of information. In his version, he was always the victim.

I flip through stacks of files, pulling out Devante's interview notes. Skimming the pages for Billy Ray's name, I only find him mentioned a couple times in passing, things Mickey claimed were unfair, where Billy Ray got special treatment. Apparently Mickey didn't go into the real details about his younger stepbrother to Devante either. A bully never likes someone who will stand up to them.

I read more of Dixie's testimony. Billy Ray took to carrying a pocketknife, even though Mickey claimed to not be afraid of him. Dozens of times, as stated by Dixie, Billy Ray came to the sisters' rescue. There were times he protected them from Mickey's mother as well, who doled out harsh beatings and other disciplines to humiliate them if they upset her.

By the time of Mickey's trial, his mother was dead, and his stepfather had suffered a stroke, leaving him unable to testify. Bonnie had married and moved to Washington State, to which she returned immediately after her turn on the stand. So much for a family reunion.

After graduating high school, Dixie attended night school in Alexandria while working as a retail clerk at Walmart. At the trial, she claimed to have trouble sleeping due to constant nightmares.

Billy Ray tried community college, then technical school. By the time his stepbrother was on trial as a serial killer, he'd worked half a dozen jobs, from mechanic to construction worker.

Where were they now?

I do an internet search on Dixie first. Google doesn't offer much outside a couple addresses where she and the others lived as kids. I browse the most popular social media platforms, but she is absent.

I search for Bonnie and find her still residing in Washington State. By the look of her Facebook profile, she's added two kids, a dog, and a horse to her family. In her picture, she looks happy. I hope she is.

Billy Ray is like Dixie—almost nonexistent in general searches and social media sites.

I log into my background check account and start plugging in names. Dixie is still in Arlington and working for Walmart, but she's been married and divorced. She has a couple speeding tickets, nothing of interest. I write down her number to give her a call later. It might not go well, depending on how much she's followed the news, but I have to try. Even though Mickey's name hasn't come up yet in the press releases, the whole situation is bound to resurrect bad memories for her.

Billy Ray's check shows he moved to the Smoky Mountains after the trial. He went off-grid after that, not so much as a rental agreement or a voter registration card showing up in the database. A part of me wonders why; the other part understands. What those kids endured at Mickey's hands—and then, as young adults, to realize he'd become a serial killer? All of them need psychological help. No wonder Dixie continued to have nightmares as an adult.

The shadows have grown deep around me, the storm outside cutting off sunlight. I get up and stretch, wondering how much longer I'll be here by myself. My fingers itch to text Meg, but she'd probably ignore me. Or tell me to quit hovering. She's probably gone somewhere for lunch. My mind plays out a scenario while thinking about Bonnie, Dixie, and Billy Ray. What would I have done in that situation to protect Meg? To protect myself?

I shudder and shove my desk back into the office. I haven't heard from Matt and text him. No answer, so I assume he's driving. I sigh, tossing the cell on the desk.

I need to do something, not just sit here and keep reading reports, but there is literally nothing I can do. I think about going to the shooting range or gym, but neither holds appeal. A niggling in the back of my brain tells me I've missed something. The clues are all here in front of me, but I can't see them clearly.

I go to the conference room, set up a fresh murder board, and start laying out a timeline with the details of Mickey's life on top, then our current serial killer running parallel below his.

I lose track of time, and the chiming of the back door opening makes me nearly jump out of my skin. Shit. I left my gun on my desk.

It's Matt, though, not the killer.

"Whoa," he says, stopping in the doorway and scanning the lines dotted with pictures, dates, and my scribbled notes. I've used different colored markers and threads to link certain things together. Meg has her form of art, I have mine. "That's impressive."

I cap one of the dry erase markers and toss it on the table. "I take it you didn't find anything at Devante's?" He would've called if he had, but I can still hope.

"He's clean. I even checked for loose floorboards and secret panels. I couldn't find anything that suggests he even watches crime shows, much less kills people."

"Then what is his fascination with Mickey? Why pick him to do a doctorate thesis on?"

"A lot of people are fascinated with serial killers. It doesn't mean they want to be one."

I contemplate picking up the marker and throwing it at him. Not because he's being snarky, but because I'm so frustrated. "Damn it."

He drags out a chair and slouches into it, kicking his feet up on another while motioning at my board. "Let's talk it out. Walk me through what you've got."

Matt would be like Billy Ray, protecting me and Meg against any threat. He isn't just a good guy, he's one of the best. He knows I need to act, to feel like I'm accomplishing something.

I walk to the board and start talking. A little while later, Meg slips in and pulls out a chair as well. The look on her face tells me not to ask questions about her visit to the morgue, so I keep going with the murder board and facts.

I'm bringing them up to speed on Mickey's stepsiblings, when JJ calls.

I hold my breath as I answer, and it rushes out of me when he tells me why he's calling.

His voice is tired, strained. "We found Devante."

19

MEG

*A*s much as I despise admitting weakness, the visit to the morgue drained me. Sucked every drop of my energy. Young women are dying and all we can do is sit around a table and talk. Talk, talk, talk.

The only thing JJ can tell us is our main suspect has a rock solid alibi. Devante, the kid who disappeared on us right after the latest murder, is apparently not our killer.

He's a college student partying in Atlanta with his fraternity brothers.

Great. Excellent. Our one solid lead collapsed under the colossal weight of this damned case. Yes, I'm irritable. Shoot me.

If the strain, that carefully crafted cadence, in JJ's words is any indication, I'm not the only crabby one. The low murmur in his voice is downright scary. I've seen him in court. He's the affable, charming guy who happily leads witnesses into corners they don't know exist. They're too busy being wooed.

Right now? Those traits are in a tight race with exhaustion.

"According to the M.E," JJ says via the speaker on Charlie's cell phone, "our vic died around midnight. Devante was in Atlanta by then. He blew you off and hopped on a six-thirty flight out of Dulles. Upon questioning, he stated he and three other guys had dinner and went to a club after checking into their hotel."

"Have you verified that?"

There's a pause and I silently wince while Matt slowly shakes his head. I recognize the silence. It's an overworked JJ battling his emotions and the unintended insult I've thrown.

"Meg," he says, his voice sharp enough to slice me in two, "are you serious right now? Of course I did. There's security video at the club. Devante and his buddies strolled right in. They left at one-fifty so unless he's Superman, there's no way he could've slipped out of the club to be in D.C. at midnight. It's a dead end."

I lean across the table and take the phone out of Charlie's hand to ensure he hears me. "JJ, I'm sorry. That came out all kinds of wrong."

"Bet your ass it did. We're all working hard."

"I know. I let my pissiness take over and that's not fair to you. It'll never happen again. I really am sorry."

Charlie waggles her fingers in a *gimme* gesture, so I hand the phone back. She'll diffuse the situation. It's a gift she has and considering she knows JJ way better than I do, I'm perfectly happy to let her intervene and do her magic.

She holds it closer to her mouth. "Mr. State's Attorney, give Meg a break and forgive her or she'll be freaking out all night over you being mad at her. We have more important things to do."

My sister meets my eye across the table and winks. In spite of myself, I can't help but smile. Charlie gets off on moments like this. They give her power, a need to conquer I will never understand or particularly crave.

"Hell, yes, I'll forgive her," JJ says. "I'm not that much of an asshole."

"Excellent." Charlie flips open a folder on the table. "Since Devante is a bust, let's move on. I've been researching Mickey's family life."

JJ groans. "Helluva mess there."

"Indeed. We should talk to his stepsisters. The stepbrother sounds like a peach also."

Curious, I grab one of the folders and skim the first page. Devante's notes on Mickey. The stepsiblings challenged him in every way. Or maybe it was the reverse and Mickey did so to the point Billy Ray took to carrying a knife.

How twisted were these people that one felt the need to be armed?

I hold the page up. "The stepbrother?"

"Yes," Charlie says. "He protected the girls. JJ, have you talked to the sisters?"

"Not yet."

At this, I'm already out of my seat, folder in hand and heading for the door.

"Meg?" Charlie calls. "What are you doing?"

"We need to talk to the family. Who's coming?"

"I'm out," Matt says. "Gotta check in with our paying clients."

"I can't," JJ says. "I have a meeting with the AG in an hour. Will you two be all right on your own?"

The Attorney General. On a Sunday. *That* can't be good.

Charlie nods. "We'll be fine. From my research, it looks like Dixie still lives in the area. Meg and I will talk to her and call you when we're done."

"All right. Be careful. And good luck. You'll need it with this bunch."

We arrive in Arlandria, a diverse multi-cultural neighborhood nestled on the border of Arlington and Alexandria counties, just before noon. As usual, JJ came through and supplied Dixie's address, which appears to be an apartment over a Peruvian restaurant. All I know is I haven't eaten yet today, and we'll be stopping for a to-go order before leaving.

Assuming she's even home. For this house call, Charlie favored the drop-in-unannounced strategy in an effort to avoid potential witnesses playing hide and seek with us.

We snag street parking and walk by a series of two-story connected brick buildings that boast a bar, a small Latino food market, and the restaurant. On the far end of the latter is a door marked 2A, B, and C. Charlie checks and finds it unlocked then opens it to reveal a set of stairs.

We're looking for 2A, so we make our way up while the aroma of cooking meat and rich spices make my stomach howl.

"When did you eat last?"

I wince and curse myself because I know what's coming and Charlie's lectures on proper nutrition can be epic. Absolutely turn-me-to-stone harsh. In light of that, I choose not to answer.

"Meg!"

"I know, I know. When we're done, we'll stop and grab something."

"You're unbelievable. One day you'll fall over."

Probably. But it won't be today so I can't worry about it now.

Charlie reaches the top and points at the first door on the left. "Here we go." She knocks lightly and puts her ear to the wood. "Movement. Bingo."

Anticipating the door swinging open, she steps back, faces it and straightens her shoulders.

"Who is it?" A woman calls from inside.

"Hi, Dixie. My name is Charlie Schock. I'm a private investigator working on a cold case. My sister, Meg, is with me."

"What do you want with me?"

"We're hoping you can give us some information about Mickey."

The long, ensuing pause is interrupted by my rumbling stomach. My sister gives me the side eye, reminding me she has issues with my lack of concern for myself. What she doesn't understand is it's not that I don't care, but it's damned difficult to stop and nourish myself when there are dead women who deserve justice.

"As soon as we're done here," she says, "you're eating. I don't care if I have to shove it down your throat."

A second later, Dixie's door swings open, revealing a woman in her late thirties with shoulder length auburn hair set off by crystalline blue eyes. Wisps of cloudy gray float between the auburn strands giving a tonal effect that provides warmth.

"Hey." Her gaze shoots to Charlie and her elegant clothing, then to me in my ripped jeans and Wonder Woman T-shirt. "Sisters, huh?"

I smile at that. "I know. Hard to believe."

I hold my hand out. "I'm Meg. Thank you for opening up."

"Sure. But I'm on my way to an appointment. Got two minutes. What do you want to know about Mickey?"

Interesting. She opened it but won't invite us in.

Charlie nods. "As I said, we're investigating a cold case. We suspect the woman was murdered by a serial killer."

Dixie's demeanor, her entire body really, seems to collapse, just fold in on itself. "Oh, God. Please tell me they didn't find more of his victims. He's the devil himself. Pure evil."

"The case we're working doesn't match up with Mickey's timeline. He was already in prison when this girl was murdered. The manner of death fits though."

"You think it's a copycat?"

I cock my head, more than likely giving away my surprise

the sister of a serial killer would automatically jump to that idea. Charlie will give me grief for, as they say in baseball, tipping my pitches, but that's me. I wear my emotions like a Burberry overcoat worth showing off.

"We don't know," Charlie says. "The killer knows a lot about Mickey's methods. We're hoping you can tell us about his friends, people he interacted with, coworkers."

"Ha," she barks. "Mickey didn't have friends. He's too much of an asshole. Nobody wanted to be near him. Except us. We were stuck with him."

"We?" I ask.

"Yeah. Myself, Billy Ray, and Bonnie, my brother and sister. Bonnie hightailed it to the other side of the country to get away from Mickey. Me and Billy Ray? We wouldn't leave. This is our home. We like the East Coast and I'm not letting that no-good monster wreck it for me. As long as Mickey is locked up, I'm staying."

Charlie leans casually against the doorjamb. "I read his trial transcripts. I'm sorry for what he put you through."

"It is what it is. We had Billy Ray. He took care of us. Mickey used to beat him senseless. Call him a useless piece of shit, but he always protected us." Dixie turns and holding the door open with her foot, reaches for something inside. The sound of jingling keys cues us that we're losing her. "I gotta go. You can walk out with me and we'll talk."

"Thank you," Charlie says. "Where is Billy Ray now?"

"He lives in the Smoky Mountains. After the trial, he got sick of the news media. Plus, his fiancée dumped him. He hid the whole Mickey thing from her and refused to go to court because he didn't want her to know they were connected."

"He lied to her," Charlie says.

"Can you blame him? Would you marry a man whose brother is a murderer?"

Point there.

Dixie nudges her chin and Charlie and I move aside to give her room. "Losing her destroyed him. All that time he'd spent protecting us, doing the right thing, sacrificing and she dumped him. Still breaks my heart. He wanted to get out of town, so he bought a cabin and hid out." She shrugs. "He liked it there and stayed."

She steps between Charlie and I to lock the door and we inch backward, in case she, like Billy Ray, likes her space. "I do know," I say. "When life gets crazy I have a spot on the Silver Tail I like. It's quiet. Babbling water, tweeting birds, swishing trees. There's something about nature that relaxes me."

"Well, you and Billy Ray would get along then. He's a nature buff."

Dixie heads for the stairwell with Charlie and I in tow. She's clipping along, but her much shorter legs are no match for Charlie. I take up the rear, more than happy to let my sister do her thing and squeeze whatever info she can from Dixie.

Charlie grabs the handrail as she hustles down, an impressive feat in her skinny, high-heels. "Do you have his address?"

"Yeah. It's a cabin off Cove Mountain Trail. In Little Greenbriar."

"Little Greenbriar?"

"East Tennessee. Deep in the mountains." She rattles off an address, then, "The cabin has a giant wagon wheel in front. You can't miss it."

Dixie pushes the door open allowing a burst of sun to light the shadowed hallway. Once we clear the doorway, she lets the door go and it closes with a loud thunk.

I hold my hand out. "Thank you, Dixie."

"You're welcome. Just don't tell Mickey I talked to you. I don't want my name anywhere near him."

Charlie says her goodbyes, offering a business card in case Dixie needs anything. I suspect what she needs is to be left alone and never hear her stepbrother's name again.

We stand under the streaming sunlight as Dixie hustles to catch a bus rolling to a stop at the corner.

"Billy Ray," I say.

Charlie spins around and heads for the Peruvian restaurant. "We'll get your food to go."

20

I feel like I'm in a time capsule, a history lesson unfolding under me as JJ and I land in eastern Tennessee. The Smoky Mountains earned their name from the fog that hangs over them, and before we touch down at the Pigeon Forge airfield, I see as many fields and forests as I have towns and Metropolitan cities.

Meg was exhausted, even after I fed her, and decided to stay home. I was going to suggest she do that anyway, but she came to the idea on her own, saving me an argument. Thank God. She pushes too hard, forgetting to eat, tossing and turning at night. Sometimes, her art helps get rid of her demons, and others, there's nothing in the world that can. I told her she needs a hobby, a boyfriend, something to bring light and joy into her world, but she claims art is all she needs. Right now, with all these dead bodies, she's draining herself to the point of a nervous breakdown.

I reminded her Matt needed help picking out a diamond for Taylor, but he's out of town for the day, working on another case, so not much help in the distraction category.

Luckily, JJ was more than happy to offer to help with the

serial killer investigation. Law enforcement has no further leads, and someone higher up and in charge of a helicopter, wants this resolved. Fast.

I admit I was relieved to not have to make the sixteen hour round-trip drive on my own. This was more of a long shot than trying to get Mickey to stop hiding behind his attorney and talk to us again, but I have a tickling in my gut that won't wait for Mickey to come down off his high horse.

While his sisters were victims, Billy Ray knows his step-brother better than anyone, I'm betting. Maybe it was only because Billy Ray wanted to keep the girls safe, and he never intended to become a hero, but looking at it from a psychological standpoint, he subconsciously understood his brother's neurosis and how to stand up to him. That may offer a key as to how I can handle this copycat.

I suspect Billy Ray will want nothing to do with us. He won't want to discuss Mickey, their childhood, or the trial, and I can't blame him. Mickey destroyed his life. Why relive that destruction? All I can do is hope he'll tell me something I don't already know that might let me peek inside the mind of this copycat killer.

Some serials pattern themselves after others they admire. They find inspiration in these "role models," studying their methods and avoiding their mistakes. I wrote an article for *Psychology Today* a few years ago about copycats and two had been so confident, so egotistical, they called in their crimes to the press to ensure investigators would make the link to their "murder mentors." They wanted credit for being better and smarter than the killer they copied.

Both were caught.

Unfortunately, there is an abundance of these role models for them, from H. H. Homes in the nineteenth century to modern-day killers like Ted Bundy–and our illustrious Mickey

Wilson. People like Devante are fascinated with him, and apparently, so is our copycat.

After landing, we hit the rental company inside the terminal. JJ and I didn't talk in the helicopter, but now I'm going to be stuck in a car with him as we venture to Cove Mountain where Billy Ray has tried to disappear.

I hold up my phone so JJ can see the screen showing my GPS map. "It's thirty-four minutes to the mountain, and at least another half hour to get to Billy Ray's place. I'm guesstimating, since GPS can't actually locate his address."

"I'll drive. You navigate."

These are our strong suits. If only our personal relationship worked so easily.

Any worries I have over JJ wanting to discuss us are put to rest when he asks me to tell him about Mickey's trial. I have the transcripts with me, so I start reading as he drives toward the giant mountains rising into the clouds in front of us.

Maybe because he's looking for tiny clues that might be revealed from the trial, or he's just tired, he listens without interrupting. Here and there I've made notes in the margins, but I stick to reading the transcript only and leave out my thoughts about the things that send up red flags. My intuition insists our copycat attended the trial.

The road becomes a two-way, the incline steepens. We pass what's considered a village too small to even register as a town. Pastures with horses, traditional farmhouses and white picket fences. It seems like every few miles there's a historical marker about a battle scrimmage or other important landmark. Signs pop up a few times, directing us to more historical places if we want to turn off the main road.

The higher we climb, the more we leave civilization behind, giant firs and oak trees creating a canopy above our heads. The GPS directs us to a turn that lands us on a gravel road. My ears pop from the pressure as we continue, snaking around bends, heading down into a valley before climbing once more.

The forest closes in, cutting off sunlight. I stop reading, but JJ doesn't say anything, either concentrating on driving or turning over Mickey and our copycat in his head.

I glance at him from the corner of my eye and see the stubborn set of his jaw. The kind of pressure he's under takes someone of extreme fortitude. I let him continue his mental stewing in silence, only offering directions when necessary. A part of me wishes this was the way it could be for us all the time —working cases side-by-side, and not having to worry about our personal relationship.

We come to a dead end out of the blue, and JJ slams on the brakes. "What the...?"

He gives me a hard look and I shrug. "I told you GPS couldn't track the exact location. It doesn't seem to exist on the map."

JJ puts the vehicle in park. "You stay here. I'll have a look around."

Meg used to make me tromp around the woods with her when we were little. I don't exactly hate it, but I find nature to be...messy. Bugs and snakes are one thing, but hell, in these woods? There are bears and cougars. Not just messy, downright dangerous.

There's no way I'm letting JJ treat me like a diva, though. I made sure to wear hiking boots in case this sort of thing happened, and, as he bails out, I follow.

He doesn't waste his breath arguing, just shakes his head, and says, "Which way?"

From my estimate, Billy Ray's should be over the next hill. I spot a foot path a few feet away. "There. Let's follow that."

It disappears in places as we hunt for it in the overgrowth. We trudge through dead leaves and forest debris, over fallen limbs and around large rocky outcroppings. A few birds sing above us and the rustling in the detritus warns me of small creatures scurrying away from our footsteps.

Small creatures I can handle. Most of them, anyway. "I hope there aren't snakes," I say, knowing it's a stupid comment. Of course there are, and my hand lightly touches the butt of my handgun at my waist for reassurance.

"I'll protect you," JJ says, making fun of me and cupping my elbow.

A lot of help he'd be against a bear or mountain lion. "Good thing I have my gun."

He grins and something smolders in his eyes. Alpha male all the way. "You don't think I can protect you?" he asks.

"Have you ever seen a bear up close? Growing up near the woods, every once in a while a bear would pay us a visit. Come on the back porch and try to get in the screen door. Wrecked everything in sight. Trust me when I say, we don't want to run into one out here."

I'm slightly out of breath from the climb and stop for a moment, the smell of pine filling my nostrils. A light mist has begun to fall. So much rain this week. "Why the hell would anyone want to live in a place this secluded?"

"Makes a good place to bury bodies," JJ jokes.

At least, I think he is, but I realize, maybe that's one of the reasons I don't like the woods. It's not only nature and wild animals that give me the creeps, I feel like a stupid heroine in a horror flick. The sinister killer is going to pop out from behind a tree at any moment.

JJ and I make it to the top of a hill, and I swear the temperature has dropped ten degrees since we climbed out of the car. My lightweight spring jacket isn't enough to block the chill and shivers run down my spine. Below, through another thicket of trees, there's a cabin. A barely visible fog floats around it and a small outhouse.

I spot the large wagon wheel Dixie described. On the north

side of the house is a pile of stacked wood, but there is no smoke coming from the stone chimney. No lights shining through the windows. There's a drive that leads in the opposite direction we came from—probably a different way, an *easier* way, to get to this place without walking through the woods.

There's no vehicle parked in the drive—if you can call the dirt road leading to the cabin that—just a four-wheeler sitting on the side, the tires caked in dried mud.

No dogs raise an alert as we make our way down the hillside. It's muddy here, and my boots slide on the wet leaves. I nearly end up on my backside, but in true alpha-male-protector form, JJ manages to grab my arm and keep me from going down. The hem of my pant legs are wet and crusted with dirt and pine needles. Definitely have to send them to the cleaners when I get home.

We slow at the edge and JJ stops me. "Let's assume Billy Ray is armed and probably doesn't like strangers showing up out of the woods at his house. I don't want to die out here from a misunderstanding."

Good thought. "Maybe we should circle around and approach from that direction."

"Maybe you should stay here and let me go talk to him."

"Fat chance. This is my lead, my idea. Besides, he's less likely to be on guard against a woman. Like you, he seems to have a protective streak toward us. All I have to do is let him know Dixie sent me."

JJ is silent a moment, stewing it over. "Yeah, no. I'm not letting you approach alone."

I start moving south toward the dirt drive. "You're just afraid to stay here and take your chances with the bears," I tease.

JJ follows. "Damn straight, I am."

I wait until we get to the drive to say what I'm thinking. "He's not here. There's no vehicle, lights, or smoke from the fireplace."

"He could be nearby, hunting or whatever guys like this do out here alone."

We're standing in plain sight, and I stare at the windows, seeing no movement of curtains. "Guess there's only one way to find out."

I keep my hands loose at my sides and call, "Billy Ray? I'm a friend of Dixie's. She sent me to talk to you."

I almost ask permission to move forward, but instead, I wait. There's no reply, still no visible movement inside. I call out again, repeating what I said, and walk slowly toward the front porch. JJ stays a few steps behind me, and I sense he is watching the woods as well as the house.

Smart man.

We spend a few more minutes trying to make sure Billy Ray isn't playing possum. Eventually, we're at the door. I look at JJ and he shrugs.

We didn't come all this way to turn around and head back to D.C. without getting something for our troubles.

I knock loudly and step back. "Billy Ray? My name is Charlize Schock and I'm looking into a copycat killer I believe is using Mickey Wilson as his mentor. I know you don't want to talk about him or what he did to your sisters, but young women are dying because of this guy. If you could answer a few questions, give me five minutes, it could save lives."

Nothing. The rain begins to fall harder. JJ motions me off the porch, signals he's going to walk around the house, peek into windows.

I keep talking, practically begging Billy Ray to help us. Finally, I stop wasting my breath. He's not here.

Dammit all to hell.

JJ finishes walking around. He shakes his head at my questioning gaze when he emerges on my left. "Could be he went to town, or maybe he hasn't been here in a long time. What do you want to do, Charlie? Wait and see if he comes home?"

I bite the inside of my bottom lip, tapping my foot on the ground and cursing silently. My hair is already soaked, and rivulets of water run down my neck, under the collar of my jacket. I stomp up the front steps once more and grab the door-knob, jiggling it. It's locked. No surprise.

I step back and give it a hard kick. The wood groans slightly, but the lock doesn't give.

"What the hell are you doing?" JJ asks.

I motion at him to come up. "Help me kick this door open."

"You want a US Attorney to break into a guy's house with no provocation?"

I hate breaking the law, but on the other hand, innocent women are dying, and I have to stop the man killing them. "I'm feeling sick, really sick, probably picked up something in the woods and I could die. You don't know what's wrong with me, and I can't make it back to the rental car. You need to get me inside, warm me up, make me tea or...something."

A muscle in JJ's jaw works. He's trying not to smile as he curses under his breath. "What do you think you're going to find in there?"

"A notepad and pen and leave this guy a message. One way or another, I'm going to talk to him. We can drive back to town and I'll find a hotel. You head back to D.C., but I'll stay here and see if I can meet him face-to-face and get something—anything—that'll help us."

The tingle in my gut is working overtime. JJ's phone rings, the soft buzzing foreign in the noise of this forested area. I'm shocked he has service at all. He pulls it out, stalling me and my break-in, to answer. I walk to the nearest window and try to peek in, but the closed curtains mostly block the view of what lies inside. I cup my hands around my eyes and stare harder. A table under the window. A rifle lies on it, three hunting knives, steel gleaming even in the shadows, on newspaper next to it.

"Yeah...when was that?" JJ's tone makes me turn to him. The

hair on the back of my neck stands up at the look on his face. "You're sure? Okay, thanks."

He disconnects and pockets the phone. Walks up onto the porch to the front door.

Something has changed—he's ready to bust it down.

"What is it?" I ask. "Who was that?"

"I asked the warden to look up all the times Billy Ray, or the sisters, visited Mickey."

"And?"

He wiggles his fingers at me. "Give me your gun."

I hand it to him, and he points it at the spot where the lock is. "Billy Ray visited Mickey in prison three days ago."

The tickle turns into a full blown cramp. "Holy shit," I say. "Do you think...? There are three knives on the table in there."

Probable cause. We don't want our search thrown out of court just in case.

He doesn't say anything, and I jump back and cover my ears as JJ fires at the door.

Inside, rain drips off the sleeves of my jacket and I pull up short only a few steps in. A wall covered in newspaper clippings and photos grabs my attention, horror slamming into me. They're from Mickey's trial, but it's the photos that make me gag and run back outside to vomit in the yard.

The majority of serial killers like to kill close to home. In this case, it appears ours prefers to do so near his *childhood* home.

I hear JJ's voice as he makes the appropriate calls to law enforcement, cursing at the shitty reception, but managing to get through. My fingers shake as I pull out my cell to call Meg.

I have no bars, no connection.

I go inside and find JJ using the landline in the kitchen, not his cell.

"Get off," I say, and when he doesn't do it fast enough, I yank the handset from him and start dialing.

Meg's goes to voicemail, and I swear softly, but I leave her a message, relaying the news.

Billy Ray has pictures of dead women plastered all over his cabin.

Worse, he also has some of two women who aren't dead yet.

Me and Meg.

21

*T*he lack of sleep finally hit me.

I'm in my studio, Avery in front of me. I've placed the tissue depth markers on the cast and started layering various sized strips of clay by her haunting blue eyes, along her brow bone and jaw. Between the strips, the pale skull peeps out, intensifying the contrast of the darker clay.

As honorable as my profession is, I'm staring at something out of a freak show. No one, cast or not, should ever have to look like this. Half complete, bulging eyeballs and giant teeth that without flesh around them are menacing choppers ready to carve me apart. She won't always look this way, but at this moment I can't stand it.

Right now this girl is an art project.

Tragic.

A raging burn licks up my spine, searing my skin from inside out. I can't move. I want to, I know I have to, but my brain and fingers can't get their shit together and connect. I've suddenly forgotten how to sculpt, and it terrifies me.

I step back, draw a long breath of stale, closed-in office air.

"I'm being an idiot," I say.

Rational Meg knows it. Sleep-deprived Meg? Not so much. She loves poking the gremlins that wait, deep inside where that fire burns, ready to remind me of my fears, failures and disappointments.

Avery and her dead eyes being one of them.

My chest collapses, just a brutal crush of bone against my lungs.

I turn from her—I have to—and stumble from my office.

No air. I need air.

"Charlie!"

My sister. She'll offer refuge. Talk me from the ledge I want to throw myself off because this will never stop. Ever. There will always be cold cases and dead people. Young women, old men, *children*. A fucking marching band of skulls in and out of my studio, silently begging for help.

I reach the hallway and prop my hand against the wall. *Air.* The pressure in my chest is too much. Too constricting. My ears fill with some kind of quasi roar-whoosh that knocks me off balance and sends me wobbling. Irrational Meg begs for darkness, for the bliss of denial that'll come when I pass out.

Please.

I don't fight it.

I need the break. Just a few seconds. Anticipating the plunge, I put my back flush against the wall and slide to the floor.

"Charlie!"

No answer. I shake my head. *Stupid girl.* I know she's not here. She's with JJ questioning Billy Ray.

The name douses the burning panic shredding me. He'll have answers and help us figure this out. Find this lunatic dumping young women along the Beltway. He has to.

I stare at the wall across from me and focus on Billy Ray as a potential lead.

The pressure in my chest eases and I squeeze out a short,

choppy breath. Then another. On my third I fill my lungs, force myself to count to three as I exhale. My vision clears and the red slashes in the painting on the opposite wall come into sharp focus.

Rational Meg suggests I've just had the mother of all panic attacks, something not exactly foreign to me, but it's been a long time, fourteen months to be exact and I'd started to believe I'd licked that little disorder.

Work. That's what I need. To ignore my scattered thoughts and push through. When I finish Avery, I'll have that sense of completion I desperately need.

I get to all fours then rise to my feet, stumbling the short distance to my office. My eyes are on the back door and I take a second to think that through. Quiet surrounds me, nipping at the back of my neck because I'm alone in this office. Security system notwithstanding, we had a break-in. And an attack on Haley. We wouldn't let her stay here alone, but somehow it's all right for Charlie and me to.

I drag my gaze and peer in at Avery.

No.

Not Avery. A reconstruction of Avery.

Who am I kidding?

Time and again I get emotionally attached to replicas—not even the real skulls—of dead people. Those reconstructions might not all be in my studio anymore, but each enters with an energy attached that never leaves. The room or me. Those we can't identify—and as good as we are, there've been a lot—their souls stick around, latch on to me like a lifeline I can't give them.

Even standing in the hallway, if I look hard enough, I can see them, sense them pulling me back into my studio, my own personal hell, begging me to find them.

And bring them home. The pressure in my chest builds. *It's happening. Again.*

I can't do it. Not so soon after the last attack. I'll go insane if I don't get control of myself. Intellectually, I understand this and I'm grateful for that clarity of mind. Moving quickly, my eyes on the floor, away from anything that might intensify my panic, I step into my office, grab my purse and sketchpad and flat-out sprint to the back door. I'm alone and I know what I need.

Still, I give Avery a silent apology, promising I'll be better in a couple hours. After a visit to my happy place.

I lock the door behind me and use the remote on my keyring to arm the security system.

I hit the Beltway and chop the sixty minute drive to the Silver Tail River in half. I don't have time to mess around with panic attacks. I'm on a mission to get my mojo back. To sit on the ground and dig my fingers into earth, inhaling the loamy scent of soil.

I check my rearview, making sure I haven't been tailed by whoever the psycho is messing with us. I even punch the gas and cross two lanes to get to my exit and let out a breath when I'm neither crushed by an oncoming truck or followed. I'm alone. *Thank you.*

After parking in my usual spot in the small gravel lot beside the kayak launch, I toss my purse in the back, hiding it under a jacket I keep there. Phone? I glance at the cupholder where I usually stow my cell. Empty. Dammit. In my rush to get here, I left it in my office. Nothing to be done about it now and berating myself won't help. Instead, I grab my supplies. Thirty minutes. That's all I need.

There are no cars aside from mine and as I glance around, I see no one. Perfect. I hop out of the van, lock it up and shove my keys in my jacket pocket. The babbling sound of water against rock immediately snaps my brain to a better place. A kinder, gentler one, as my sister liked to joke.

Good. This is good.

Thirty minutes and back to work I go.

I stride along the old dirt path formed from years of residents in my hometown trudging along. Two hundred yards ahead is the old shack—the she-shed.

As I pass, I don't fight the smile. It contributed to my love of the outdoors and I'd spent plenty of nights lying on the tiny front deck staring at stars with my family. Charlie had even secretly brought a few boyfriends to the shed. Even then, my sister was a forward thinker.

Me? This was *my* place. I wasn't about to share it with someone who'd probably break my heart. Looking back, my memories here only include happy, carefree moments and that's what I need now.

It's been years since I've been inside, but from the outside, I can see edges of rotting wood. Frankly, it's a miracle the thing is still standing. A testament to Dad's woodworking skills I suppose. If I had more time, particularly today when I could use a few moments to immerse myself in the joyful times of my childhood, I'd go in and see what kind of condition the place is in.

Next time.

I keep walking, my feet crunching over loose gravel along the path. There's a giant boulder just ahead that sits at the top of the river bank. That's my spot. I like to sit on the ground, my back propped against the boulder as the water laps below me. Heaven.

My version of it anyway.

I peer up at the sun and–yay, me—I've timed this just right. At this hour, it'll shine directly on my rock, splaying its warm rays over me while I sketch.

While I work out my *issues*.

Demons, really, but that sounds so melodramatic. As if I don't have a great life. Compared to what I see on any given day, I have nothing to be wrecked over.

I climb the small hill leading to my rock and there it is, waiting for me to take my spot.

Leaning over, I pat the top of it, feel the cold, craggy surface against my warm palm. "Hello, old friend. Miss me?"

"I sure did."

I whip around and find a man fifteen feet from me. Good Lord, where the hell did he come from? He's wearing a black beanie hat, one of those plaid button-down jackets over a T-shirt and what looks to be tattered Wrangler jeans. My gaze shoots to his rubber-soled boots where a hole has worn on the right toe.

I don't recognize him, but he could be anyone. Maybe the older sibling of a schoolmate?

"Hello," I say. "Sorry. I didn't realize anyone was here."

He takes a step closer.

One.

Single.

Step.

My stomach burns like acid tearing through the lining and for the first time I realize how stupid I am.

It's the middle of the day and I'm alone in the woods with a man I don't know.

Charlie will ream me for this.

I look at my hands where the only weapons I have are my pad and pencils. And my keys.

Front pocket.

I stand still, refusing to retreat or show any fear. Predators smell it and capitalize on it. And, for all I know, this could be the guy who plays Santa at the drugstore every year.

Creepy Santa, no doubt, but still...

I shift my pencils to my other hand and slide my now free one into my jacket pocket, wrapping my fingers around my keys. Just in case.

He takes another step closer and I square my shoulders. "I'm sorry. Do I know you?"

"I think you do," he says. "I know you. Megan Eleanor Schock."

That acid in my gut churns.

Over.

And over.

And over.

I lift my chin, stare him right in the eye making sure he knows I'm not afraid to look straight at him and memorize the features of his face. The small mole below his eye, the veiny redness of broken capillaries on his nose. All of it, committed to memory.

I've never liked games. Particularly ones played by creepy men roaming the woods. I spent my adolescence worrying about guys like him.

"Ah," I say. "You know my name. Now what's yours?"

"I'm Billy Ray. I hear you've been looking for me."

"Billy Ray Carter?"

"Yes, ma'am. Dixie said you wanna talk to me. How can I help you?"

Relief takes hold. I let out a hard breath, giving my system a few seconds to unwind itself. The emotional buzz saw of the day will let me sleep for a week after this.

Jesus, the man scared me.

And what the hell is he doing here? Apparently my evasion skills need work because he had to have followed me. Regardless of our intent to question him, did he not think it a tad bizarre to tail me?

"Billy Ray, how did you get here?"

"Well, I was about to visit your office. I saw you leave so..."

He shrugs and doesn't bother to finish his sentence.

This is a weird dude. That's all I can think. Cagey? Or just socially inept?

Maybe both given his family history. Charlie would know better than me. All I know is the relative of a serial killer followed me to the woods and I'm alone with him. Excellent.

"We're investigating a cold case. We believe there's a copycat of your stepbrother's modis operandi—mode of operation."

"A copycat? He must be a sick fucker then."

"It appears so. Dixie said Mickey didn't have many friends."

A burst of chilly spring wind rattles the overhead branches, shaking the leaves and Billy Ray shoves his hands in his pockets.

"Nobody could stand him," he says. "Mean as the day is long."

"Do you remember anyone else who might've been around? Anyone he may have shared information with?"

A slow smile reveals yellowed teeth that could use a trip to the dentist.

Weird.

Dude.

He moves his right hand, drawing it, inch by inch, from his pocket. The edge of something wooden peeps out from beneath his closed hand and my ears roar.

"Billy Ray? What do you have there?"

He takes a step forward and I take one back, retreating as I keep my gaze on him. "What is that?"

He stops moving. "You asked who Mickey told stuff to."

"Yes. Do you remember anyone?"

"Yeah," he says, his smile widening. "Me."

Then he lifts his hand, showing me exactly what he'd been hiding. A garrote hangs from his fingertips.

Him.

Shit.

I focus on the cord, on his other hand gripping the end. "It's you," I blurt.

All this time, Mickey has been in jail and his stepbrother has taken up the effort.

"It's me," he says.

And then he's on me, moving so fast I barely have time for it to register. I throw my art supplies at him and use the measly second of his stunned shock to sprint left, back toward the dirt path.

I grip my keys, yanking them from my pocket and I hear Charlie's voice. *Go for the eyes. The throat. The knee.*

The crotch he'll expect. *Go there second.*

Behind me, the humph-humph of heavy breathing closes in and heat bores through me. No. Please. Not now. I focus on the she-shed—right there—while battling my rising panic.

No lock. It won't help me. And the last thing I want is to be trapped inside with a psycho kicking in the rotting door.

I pump my legs, running harder, but Billy Ray has a good twelve inches on me. His strides cover more ground and the humph-humph closes in, surrounds me. My ears whoosh and blood stretches my veins to bursting.

Breathe.

I have to or I'll pass out, fall to the ground in front of a serial killer. Charlie comes to me again.

Fight hard. Let him know you won't make it easy.

A scream leaves me. A raging, howl that shreds my throat as I run.

Oooff. Something hard smacks against the back of my head and pain spreads like a web in my skull.

"Bitch," he says.

My eyes blur and I blink, once, twice, three times. *It's coming.* The blackness.

"Goodnight, Megan Eleanor Schock.

22

CHARLIE

*M*y heart feels like it's turning inside out with fear, my pulse pumping so hard it's in a loudness contest with the helicopter's blades. *Thumpthumpthump.* Everything in me is triple-timing it, my right knee bobbing up and down, my hands sweating.

Billy Ray isn't at the cabin. He's hunting Meg. I know these two facts like I do my own birth date. JJ has tried to convince me otherwise—that Meg is fine, that Billy Ray is not in D.C—but I know better.

God help me, she might already be dead. The thought makes my guts turn over, and I clench my jaw at the threat of my empty stomach revolting once more. My sister, my friend, my partner.

How could I have let this happen? I'm trained to get inside the head of criminals, to dissect serial killers and understand them better than they do themselves. Anger pounds away alongside the fear. Anger at myself, anger at Billy Ray, anger at everyone.

JJ called in the local police and FBI to gather evidence at Billy Ray's cabin before we left. I insisted we take off before they arrived, threatening to leave him behind when he said he needed to stay and give everyone background on Billy Ray and Mickey. No way was I wasting time waiting for him when Meg's life was in danger. He acquiesced and a state trooper met us at the base of the mountain and escorted us with lights flashing to the airfield. On the way, JJ called the D.C. police, instructing them to put out an APB on Billy Ray's vehicle, and to be on the lookout for Meg's van as well.

Too slow. Everything is taking too much time. I've called Meg a dozen times, all going straight to voicemail. She has her phone turned off, I'm sure of it, which means I can't trace it. I've called everyone I can think of to ask if they've seen her, even Dr. Gentry. No luck.

Matt is out of town on a case, but I called him anyway, and he's on his way back to the office. I saw on the security system app that Meg left, but. I instruct Matt to go there anyway. Maybe she left a note.

Matt, too, has tried to convince me she's fine. "Meg is smart. She's not going to let a killer sneak up on her."

She *is* smart, but I can't reach her. I know when my sister's in trouble, and she is in big trouble right now.

Matt put in a call to Taylor and her FBI cohorts are also looking for Billy Ray. I called my parents, but they aren't home. Mom owns a cell phone but rarely turns it on. I keep praying Meg simply took my advice and went home for a nap.

Please let her be sleeping safely in her bed.

The fear screaming through my system tells me that's a pipe dream.

I will kill him. If Billy Ray lays one hand on my sister, I will kill him.

I'm usually rational in a crisis, levelheaded. It's one of my skills. Nothing rattles me. But right now? I'm a basket case. This is my fault for not seeing what was right in front of my eyes.

We're nearing D.C. when JJ reaches over and pulls my shaking hand into his. I'm praying by the time we land, one of us will receive a call that the police or FBI have found Billy Ray —and Meg—safe and alive.

No such luck.

The updates from everyone are the same--both in the wind. I call Dixie, but there is no answer. Did she lie to us? Is she in on it too? JJ orders another police unit to go to her apartment and workplace to find her.

My mind circles in ever tightening loops. Where would Billy Ray take Meg?

I place a call to Grey as JJ drives us to meet Matt at the duplex. Grey is silent as I give him the scoop. "Is there any way Teeg can track her phone's GPS with it turned off?" I ask, pleading inside that he'll be able to work a miracle.

He assures me there is not. When JJ and I arrive the van isn't there. I unlock the door on her side, anyway, calling her name as I rush through the place, leaving Grey on hold. Matt arrives seconds later, and I shake my head as he comes barreling inside, JJ on his heels.

"Charlie?" Grey asks, his voice sounding a million miles away even though I have him on speaker. "Is she there?"

The panic threatens to cut off my voice. "No," I answer barely above a whisper. *I've lost her.*

I never cry, but a wave of heat rises in my face, hot tears pushing against my eyes.

"She doesn't have OnStar or LoJack on her van?" Grey asks, checking off boxes.

"The thing doesn't even have power locks." I'm still shaking but talking to Grey takes the edge off. I blink away the tears, worthless in their appearance. Matt's presence, too, helps me take a deep breath. JJ rubs my back, supportive and protective. After another breath, I look at Matt and JJ as I say to Grey, "I need some fucking suggestions."

"You know your sister better than anyone," Grey answers. "If she's not at the office or home, where would she go? Is there a grocery store? A favorite coffee shop? An art supply store or a gallery she likes to visit?"

Our parents' home. "She goes to see our mom and dad, but I've already called them multiple times and left messages on their machine. They're not home"—a horrible thought hits—

"oh shit."

What if they *are*? What if Billy Ray has...

"What?" All three men—JJ, Matt, and Grey—shout in unison.

I swallow the rough pit lodged in my throat, my hand holding the cell falling to my side. I'm shaking so hard, I don't know how my legs are holding me up, but inside I've gone very still. "What if Billy Ray has all three of them?"

JJ grabs my free hand and yanks me toward the door. "Let's go. I'll send a black and white over there. Matt, follow us."

I hear Grey's voice coming from the phone. "I'll meet you there!"

It takes twelve minutes, JJ breaking all speed limits on the way. We pull down the long drive. No van.

I curse under my breath, and in the next, pray again to whatever power might be listening.

The house is empty, the answering machine blinking with the messages I left my parents.

All the way there, I kept going over Grey's words. Where would she go if not here?

An art supply store or a gallery... I grasp my phone, open the security system app again and study her going out the back exit to get in her van. "She has her sketchpad!"

JJ and Matt look at me with confusion.

"She's gone to her happy place. In the woods!"

Relief swamps me first—she's okay. She's at the boulder, sketching. Then comes irritation—why the hell would she go off alone when a serial killer is running loose?

Panic hits again.

Meg–my sweet, gentle sister who loves nature–is alone there near our family home.

With Billy Ray hunting her.

I tear past Matt and JJ, those goddamn tears threatening once more. They follow, yelling questions in my wake.

I see the van a few steps later, partially hidden from the drive in a small clearing.

I keep running, start screaming. "Meg!"

The others join in. "Meg! Meg! Meg!" Our voices echo through the trees.

The shaking resumes when I find the big boulder–her favorite spot–empty. The sketchpad lies in the dirt. Matt picks it up, brushes if off.

"He took her into the woods." I can barely breathe. "We'll find her. We *have* to!"

Footprints. I see footprints then JJ is marching past the path, following them. He points to an area where the grass is matted down. "She fell." There's a spot of blood in the grass.

"Meg!" I scream at the top of my lungs, and then Matt is beside me.

"Is there another entrance where Billy Ray could've parked?" He asks. I can see the panic grabbing him now. See how he's also tamping it down, trying to think logically.

We haven't seen Billy Ray's truck or any other vehicle. I hang onto that last thread of hope. Meg might've fallen, sprained her ankle, bumped her head. She couldn't make it back to the house, that's all. She's probably sitting under a tree. I spin in a circle.

"The only other entrance is through these woods from the opposite side, but..."

The playhouse! I didn't even notice it when I ran down here, so intent on getting to the boulder. Maybe she went to the she-shed, as she calls it.

I run back down the path, both men trailing after me. Sure enough, I pick up footprints again, veering off the path and...

My blood turns cold.

Something was dragged through the grass toward the shed.

Not something. Some*one*.

JJ and Matt see it too. The three of us slip behind trees to follow the matted grass but stay out of sight of the shed.

JJ touches my arm. I look over to see him pointing to a truck behind a copse of trees. The license plates are Tennessee. We glance at each other, then Matt whistles softly to get our attention. Grey is coming down the barely-there path.

By the time he joins us, all my training kicks in. I'm cool, calm, the fire inside me burning fierce, but honed and ready. The woods around us are too quiet, but we pick up the sound of a man's voice coming from the shed.

Billy Ray.

JJ takes out his phone. "I'll have a hostage rescue team here in twenty," he murmurs.

Too long. "I'm not waiting." Grey, Matt, and I are armed. I hand my weapon to JJ. "Here's what we're going to do," I tell the three of them.

Billy Ray wants me, as well as my sister, right?

Well, he's about to get me, and I pray I'm not too late.

23

*M*y sister's screaming from outside has rattled my captor.

Not a good thing when the psychotic maniac wants to kill me. I mean, seriously, I don't need this wacko amped-up any more than he already is.

I'm seated on the floor, legs splayed in front of me, my pulse slamming. The seat of my jeans is damp from the mildew and wood rot underneath me and a chill shoots straight up my spine. I can't think too hard about that. I know how this goes. Mom always tells me what I focus on grows. I'll think, and think and think, and then I'll feel it, that idling panic waiting for its moment to take over. To steal my air and any ounce of sense in my head.

I glance at the broken window, currently the only light source illuminating the she-shed. As petite as I am I won't fit through it. The door, barely ten feet away, is my only option but with my hands tied behind my back I'll need Billy Ray distracted for at least a few seconds so I can maneuver to my feet. He's left them free. Why, I'm not sure, but he's far from stupid. He has a plan. One that requires them to be of use and I don't like it.

I also don't like the knife sheathed at his waist.

Another shout from outside spins him toward the entrance —*move*—and I bend my knees, readying myself to roll and hop to my feet. At least until Billy Ray angles sideways, his squirrelly gaze shooting between me and the door.

He points to said door with a trembling finger. Right now, Billy Ray is not the cold, methodical killer we anticipated. He's nervous.

Unprepared.

Anxious.

In this moment, he's more dangerous than ever.

He jabs that finger again. *Jab, jab, jab.* "Who's out there?"

I shrug. I need every mental advantage so I'm not about to tell him it's Charlie. If I know my sister, she's brought plenty of reinforcements. I just need to hope they get in here before he slices my throat open.

My chest seizes. The panic, that evil bitch inside me, is coming awake, ready to strike. I force out a slow, steady breath, then another. *I'm okay.* Once I get out of this, I can fall apart.

I peer up at Billy Ray. He's watching me, his eyes lit with smug dominance that fires something inside me. I push my shoulders back and meet his haunting gaze. *Sorry, ace.* He may have my hands tied, but I refuse to give in.

Not happening.

"Billy Ray, stop this. Whoever is out there will check the shed. Everyone knows this is my quiet place. My van is parked in its usual spot, so they know I'm here somewhere. No one will leave until they find me. You know it."

"Shut up."

"Billy Ray—"

He rushes straight at me, just an explosion of energy that snaps me back. Dammit. That flinch just gave him the power I so desperately clung to. He knows it too. Intends to capitalize, I'm sure.

Move.

I shift my weight, but he's too fast for me. His hand shoots to my neck, his rough, gnarly fingers wrapping around my throat. Huge hands. Absolute frying pans. The knife at his waist blurs my vision. This is how he does it. His victims. He waits for them to pass out then nearly decapitates them. God help me. I can't die like this.

My ears roar and the anxiety I've kept on lockdown stirs, swirling in my belly and rising. Up, up, up. Billy Ray squeezes harder, enough that my air is gone and the pressure behind my eyes builds. Then he releases me. Squeeze, release, squeeze, release.

Bastard.

"*I'm* in control," he says.

The door swings open, banging against the inside wall. A blast of light blinds me and I blink, then do it again as Billy Ray's grip eases. The infusion of air clears my vision enough to see Charlie standing there, backlit by the growing clouds behind her. Feet planted, hands on hips, she's Wonder Woman without the costume.

Billy Ray whips his head around. "Jesus."

My sister. The badass.

The sight of her shatters my panic and my lungs take in a stream of moist, mildewy air.

Charlie doesn't look directly at me. I know her. If she sees fear in me, she'll...I don't know what she'll do, but she's a pro. She knows emotional stability is imperative, so she keeps her focus on the man with his hand clamped on her sister's neck.

She holds up her hands. "I'm unarmed. But there are various branches of law enforcement surrounding us. This is over, Billy Ray. Let go of her before I unleash hell on your ass."

Ooh, good one. Way to rile up the control freak. Make him come a little unglued.

He squeezes my throat again and I struggle against his grip, attempting to pry myself loose. Not an easy task with my hands restrained, but I don't care. Charlie is here. Two against one. No matter how big he is, we outnumber him. We *will* walk out of here.

Charlie takes a step, coming closer.

Billy Ray points at her. "Stay there."

He's rattled again, sensing the situation slipping from him. I might as well push him, see if I can tap into his anger. "You have nowhere to go, Billy Ray. Charlie isn't about to let you kill me. And if you think I'll make this easy—" I finally meet my sister's gaze, "—that *we will*, you're wrong. You useless piece of shit."

His eyes flash and he squeezes again, the movement so quick, I can't react. The pressure is insane, and my throat collapses under his grip. I gag. *Too much.* I've pushed too far. In front of me, his body seems to expand, all that rage boiling up.

"Useless piece of shit," Charlie repeats, her voice smooth as custard on a summer day. "That's what Mickey used to call you."

Words piddle around in my head and I desperately try to get them in order. With my air cut off, I can't form a sentence. It's all...fuzzy. Just out of my cognitive reach.

I look straight into Billy Ray's eyes, determined not to blink back the tears. Allow myself to look more than a little desperate. If it'll distract him from Charlie, I'll give him the power.

"Useless piece of shit," Charlie says again.

She's totally fucking with him now and my oxygen-deprived brain finds this amusing.

I laugh and Billy Ray releases me with a brutal shove that sends me sideways. He swings to Charlie, his hands in motion as he reaches for his waist.

Knife!

That few seconds is all I need. I roll, somehow getting to my knees as Billy Ray unsheathes that knife and takes a step toward my sister.

A vision of Avery and Emily, their skulls on stands in my office, fills my foggy mind.

Not again. Never again.

I spring up, wobbling as I get my footing, but Billy Ray, he's in the throes of a Charlie-induced rage that has him forgetting all about little-'ol-me. He takes another step toward her, knife at the ready.

Not happening.

Never again.

Go.

In two strides I'm on him, but the realization of his circumstances hits him, and he stops, pivots back to me. *Perfect.* Before he can complete the turn, my eyes blur. It's okay. I know what I have to do, and I don't need my eyes for it. Agonizing hours of my sister's lectures and practice sessions have left me with razor-sharp instincts. I kick out, firing every ounce of hate and pain I can muster to the heel of my boot. I connect with flesh. Success. I kick again, watch as my foot bashes his crotch and the open-mouthed look on his face? The shock and pain?

Better than winning the lottery.

A vicious howl fills the air. Billy Ray screaming. My ears ring and I shake my head, force myself to focus on the man rolling on the ground holding his crotch.

I've probably crushed his balls and he didn't even see it coming.

I stand there, fists high, staring at him. Waiting for him to move so I can blast him again.

Knife.

On the floor. Next to him. What I've done, what could've happened here slams me. An absolute landslide of terror that paralyzes me.

A flash of movement catches my eye as Charlie kicks the

knife away, sending it skittering against the wall. Behind her, a rush of bodies charge through the doorway and the she-shed is suddenly filled with men in tactical gear. And JJ, Grey, and Matt.

The men in my life are all here.

Of course. They weren't about to miss this.

After all, the Schock sisters have just captured a serial killer.

24

CHARLIE

*T*wo visits to the hospital in as many days. This time, however, I'm a happy camper.

Billy Ray is in custody and my sister is safe.

Safe. The word reverberates through me as the ER doctor clears Meg to leave, asking her to follow up with our family physician. She's got a slight concussion, a few ugly bruises, and some nightmare memories to add to those already in her head, but she's alive and kicking—literally—and handled our serial killer like a trained FBI agent.

I'm damned proud of her.

"You did good, sis," I say as I wheel her down the long, antiseptic smelling hallway. She balked at leaving in a wheelchair, but that's how it works.

I've already spoken to the local cops and Matt's girlfriend, Taylor, so the FBI and detectives working on this case have the details. Billy Ray lawyered up as soon as he could talk again, thanks to Meg's crushing blow to his family jewels. According to JJ's latest text, the FBI brought Dixie in for questioning along with her brother. I'll take Meg down to the station to give our official reports first thing tomorrow. "I want to keep an eye on that concussion, so I'm taking you home with me."

She nods, silent, but I don't worry. Meg needs time to process and I'll get her to a psychiatrist friend of mine soon for some talk therapy. Another thing she'll balk at, but I'll give her the option of talking to me—as a psychologist, not her sister—or visit Paulette. I know which one she'll choose.

"I need to go to the office," she murmurs. "I need to see Emily and Avery."

That's the last thing she needs, but it will do her good to speak to her girls and tell them we've caught their killer. "Billy Ray wants a deal. He's the one who broke into your office and attacked Haley. He's also offered important details that'll help us identify them," I tell her. "JJ believes we'll have their real names by the end of the day."

Matt is at the curb waiting. He fusses over Meg, nicknaming her Suburban Commando, and doing some silly Kung Fu moves, as if demonstrating what she did to Billy Ray. She laughs at his antics and the sound helps me breathe. He picks her up and sets her inside the passenger seat of his Mustang, ignoring her protests. I hop in back and direct him to take us to the office.

He gives me a sharp look in the rearview, but I nod to let him know it's okay.

My voicemail is filled with messages, the most important from our parents. I check in to tell them Meg is okay, and I'll have her talk to them once we're settled.

Our visit to the office is brief, Meg going into her space and shutting the door. While she's in there, I return calls. Matt paces. It's getting dark outside when my phone lights up with a call from JJ—Billy Ray is talking.

I deliver the news to Meg through her closed door. I can't see her, and she doesn't make a sound for a moment after I tell her Emily and Avery are believed to be Naomi Gardiner and

ADRIENNE GIORDANO & MISTY EVANS

Elizabeth Dunhurst, but I can feel her relief as if she and the ghosts of those girls share a collective sigh.

The FBI wants confirmation, so dental records will be pulled, and they'd like Meg to finish her skull work to compare to pictures of both girls. "Of course," she says when I tell her. "Emily is already done, and I'll work through the night on Avery."

Over my dead body, but really, arguing will get me nowhere, and I know my sister. She won't sleep tonight anyway. Not until she's finished that skull.

"Okay," I say through the door. "I'll order takeout."

Matt gives me a frown. "She needs rest."

"She needs closure." I hand him some cash and the key to Meg's front door. "Would you please grab food and fresh clothes for her?"

The press hounds me for the next few hours and I stop taking calls. Grey and his wife, Sydney, show up with flowers, and a couple bodyguards to keep the reporters off our premises. I could kiss them.

Matt returns with pizza and the clothes, Taylor following. She can't stay, since her department is in charge of cold cases, but she manages to coax Meg out of her office long enough to change and talk. My sister is gracious and polite, but I see the tension in her eyes, the restrained impatience around her mouth.

Taylor recognizes it too and makes her escape. After she leaves, Meg goes back to work, but her office door stays open. Progress.

"Come have some pizza," I say to her a few minutes later from the doorway. "You'll need your strength to pull an all-nighter."

If she weren't already dead on her feet, she'd refuse. I see the wheels in her brain turn, her exhaustion and the need to wrap this up warring inside her. I don't push—that would be the wrong thing to do—and after a moment, she relents, following me to the conference room.

Matt, ever the jokester, manages to get a couple smiles out of her, and Sydney briefly relates her own experience with a serial killer. I didn't know about the incident, and we don't go into details, but it seems to give Meg a boost. She's not the only one at the table with that experience and Sydney lets her know she's available to talk if Meg ever wants to.

We are mostly through eating when JJ shows up. He makes a face at Meg's favorite Thai version, but helps himself to the last of the sausage. "Thirteen," he tells us. "We've got Billy Ray for thirteen potential missing persons cold cases, thanks to Taylor and her team. We're still working out the details of his deal, but he's already copped to three, the first he took the day after Mickey was convicted. She was his fiancée and she apparently freaked out when she discovered his stepbrother was a serial killer. They argued, she called him names and tried to bail on him. Because of Mickey. All his life he'd been dealing with him and his fallout. Just when he thought he was done with his insane relative, the lover dumps him. He lost it. Went into a rage and killed her by cutting her throat to shut her up. Claims it was an accident—some accident—but after that, he had the itch and couldn't stop. He thought moving to the boondocks, cutting himself off from the world, might work. It didn't."

Meg's eyes are cold, calculating. "What does he get in return if he confesses to all of them?"

JJ meets her stare. "Life in prison rather than the death penalty."

My sister doesn't believe in the death penalty, but I see disappointment in her eyes. We've argued over the merits of it many times, so I'm both surprised and *not*. There are certain monsters who make you question your personal codes.

JJ downs the last of his slice and turns to me. "Thank your dad for me, will you?"

"For what?"

"He found Juanita's biological cousins and they contacted her. Seems her real mother has been looking for her for about a year. He said you suspected a mix up at the hotel where Yvonne gave birth? Seems you may be right. Anyway, they're all getting together this weekend to hash things out. A family reunion of sorts. Juanita couldn't be happier to meet her *real*"—he makes air quotes—"biological mother and introduce her to Yvonne, as well as her adoptive parents."

The irony is there if you think about it. Juanita now has three mothers, even though two aren't biological. "Yvonne was so convinced Juanita was hers. Should be an interesting get together."

"You should take her on as a client," Meg says. "Help her find her real daughter."

"You're right," I say, making a mental note to contact Yvonne next week. This is why I do it—to bring lost families together again. I turn to JJ. "I'm happy for all of them."

"She'll be calling you. She wants to invite you and Meg to the reunion."

I look at Meg and she smiles at me. A real one, the old Meg surfacing. "We look forward to it."

I walk him out, both of us tired but feeling that inexplicable rush of satisfaction at having nailed Billy Ray. JJ is going to be tied up for the next several days as he heads the investigation to make sure all the I's are dotted and T's crossed.

"You gave me ten new gray hairs today," he says, brushing a kiss on my forehead. "Don't ever bust in on a serial killer again, or I will stroke out and die."

Matt said something similar to me. Grey seems to be the only one who isn't having a cow about my direct confrontation with Billy Ray. He would've done the same thing in my situation, most likely, and therefore hasn't scolded me.

"She's my sister, JJ. Billy Ray's lucky he's still alive. The only reason I didn't kill him is because I knew he had information about the victims we need to give their families closure."

JJ rubs my arm, stares at me. "You are one kick ass woman, Charlie Schock. Remind me to never get on your bad side."

I see regret cross his features, but it's gone in an instant. He *is* on there and he knows it. "Just don't mess with my sister and I won't have to kill you."

It's a joke, but it falls a little flat. Suddenly, Meg is at my side. She slides her arm through mine. "Ditto for me, JJ. Either deal with your marital situation or stop messing around with Charlie's emotions. In other words, shit or get off the pot and make her happy, or you and I will go a couple rounds."

Whoa. Both JJ and I give her a look, neither of us expecting Meg to lob threats at him. She just squeezes my arm a little tighter, a show of solidarity.

"My sister's a badass too," I say. "In case you didn't know."

For once, JJ doesn't have a response. He gives us both a nod and walks out.

"He's completely in love with you," Meg says. "Whatever he has going on with his estranged wife, he's an idiot for not pushing his divorce through."

"Thank you."

"For what?"

"For standing up for me." I turn and hug her, holding her close for longer than I normally would. I close my eyes and thank whatever gods there might be for her safe return. "I'm sorry if I scared you in the cabin. I couldn't stand outside and hope the SWAT team got there before Billy Ray killed you."

We part and she brushes a stray hair from my cheek and slips it behind my ear. "I think I was just as scared he would kill you, you brazen brat. I have to agree with JJ on this one—you ever do something foolhardy like that again, and I'll stroke out."

"No you won't. You'll kick my ass from here to hell and back."

Another real smile. "I may do that anyway."

I put my arm around her shoulders, and we walk slowly back to the conference room. Grey and Matt are telling stories to Sydney, all of them laughing. Syd looks at me as Meg and I reenter the room. "Grey claims you're almost as good of a profiler as he is. I don't buy it. I think you're better."

Ooh, fighting words. "Of course, I am," I say, adding fuel to the fire. "I'm a woman."

Matt throws up his hands. "Here we go with the feminist propaganda again."

He loves to poke fun of my views, but he supports every one of them. For the next few minutes, we continue the competitive teasing. Meg starts to float away to her office, trying to slip out quietly, but Matt calls her back. "Hey, Suburban Commando. Charlie said you want to take me shopping for Taylor's ring."

She stops in the doorway and puts a hand on her hip. "Well, someone needs to give you guidance. You don't have a clue what she'd like."

"You tell him, sister," Sydney says, nodding her head. "Every man needs a primer when it comes to picking out an engagement ring."

"Now wait a minute..." Grey sputters, Matt echoing the same sentiment. "It's a lot of pressure, you know. You all have these little quirks about what you like and don't like, and how are we supposed to know? The size, the cut...it's enough to make anyone crazy. Definitely a no-win situation."

"Exactly why you shouldn't do it on your own." Sydney pats his arm. "You need an expert."

"I'm giving the police my statement at nine a.m.," Meg tells Matt. "After that you and I are going shopping. Bring your credit card."

Matt moans softly, rolling his eyes, but the grin on his face tells me he'll do anything—including spending a small fortune —to make Taylor *and* Meg happy. This is why I love him.

Meg goes to her office. Sydney and Grey leave. Matt takes the pizza boxes out to the trash and heads home for the night. The silence is deafening, but I leave Meg alone and catch up on paperwork. I hear her classical music come on and settle into my chair.

Thank God, she's still alive.

Shortly after ten, she wanders into my office and drops into a chair. "As much as I want to do the all-nighter, my head is killing me. I've had it for today. How about you?"

I know Avery—*Elizabeth*—isn't finished yet, but I'm glad Meg's willing to call it quits for tonight. It's been a long, damn day, and I'm more than ready to close up shop. My eyes are gritty with exhaustion, my limbs heavy with fatigue. "Thought you'd never ask."

We're heading out when a young boy wheels into the parking lot on a bicycle. "Who's that?" Meg asks.

She survived an attack by a serial killer earlier today and needs a relaxing bath and twelve hours of uninterrupted sleep. I could use the same.

"No idea." I motion for her to stay at the car and grumble when she ignores me. We walk toward the kid and wait for him to shut off the bike. "Can I help you? Are you lost?" I ask.

Under the parking lot's solar lights, he looks barely old enough to be legal on that bike. Curfew's in an hour. "Are you Charlie Schock?"

The whole thing is weird and my gut tells me he's some kid with a loose screw who saw the news about us and Billy Ray Wilson and wants an interview for his class project. "We're closed. You can call our number and leave a message. We'll get back to you."

Or we won't, if you're a freak. Some days, I hate myself for being so paranoid, but it comes with the territory. I'm a former profiler for the FBI and I have a Ph.D. in forensic psychology. The list of freaks in my background is extensive.

"I left a message." He gets off the bike, releasing the kick-stand, and reaches into his jacket. "Several in fact. You didn't return any of them."

Gun. It's my first instinct when his hand goes into that jacket and I back up, putting my hand on the butt of my own weapon. At the same time, I throw the other arm out to protect Meg.

The kid pulls out a folded piece of paper, not a weapon, and holds it out to me. "I need your help."

The magic words. The ones I can never resist, especially when I move closer and see the pleading look in the kid's eyes. Maybe the shadows under them are from the ghostly lighting, or maybe he hasn't slept in a while either.

My fingers itch to reach for the paper hovering in the air between us. Meg moves so she is by my side, sizing up the boy and his paper.

"With what, kid?" I ask him, dropping my protective arm.

"I need you to explain this." He unfolds the paper and holds it out again. "I've been over these tests results a dozen times, and I understand what they mean, but they don't make sense."

I see DNA markers on the sheet. There are three sets of them. "Why is that?"

He shifts his weight, those eyes still imploring me to take the paper. "I'm Ethan Havers. Do you remember me?"

It only takes a heartbeat for the name to click and then I look the boy over from head to toe. "Carl and Lily Havers' son?"

He nods.

The first kidnapping case I caught as an FBI agent.

"Wait, Carl Havers, the morning talk show host?" Meg studies Ethan carefully. "I did the age progression on you."

Fifteen years ago, Carl was an up and coming reporter for a local DC news channel. His good looks and winning on-air personality moved him swiftly into the anchor seat, where he's been ever since. His wife, Lily, also a TV personality, gained wide audience appeal when she became pregnant with their first and only child.

"I chose to do my final project in Biology on DNA," Ethan says. "My *family's* DNA. But there's a big, big problem, Charlie."

I take the paper from Ethan's hand. A few days after he was born, he was kidnapped by his babysitter. I'm the FBI agent who returned him to his parents seven years later, after tracking down the woman. Meg did, indeed, create an age progression of what Ethan looked like at seven, and it led to me finding him. "What is it, Ethan?"

But I know what the problem is before he even answers. The DNA markers of Carl, Lily, and Ethan dance before my eyes. Meg studies them over my shoulder.

"They don't match," the kid says softly. His voice is rough, almost as if he's about to cry. "My DNA didn't come from my mom and...from *them*."

"Holy shit," Meg says.

Holy shit is right.

I look up and meet Ethan's eyes, speechless. My stomach bottoms out.

"You returned me to the wrong parents, Charlie," he whispers. "I'm not Ethan Havers."

ENJOY THIS EXCERPT FROM STEALING JUSTICE!

*J*ustice "Grey" Greystone stood in the shadows near the main staircase of the mammoth mansion, his ear bud in place, his security service badge in plain view, and his eyes roaming the crowd as senators, diplomats, and other male politicians moved past him. In a sea of navy, brown, and black suits, pops of red, pink, and bright blue caught his attention.

Beautiful women, their taut, young bodies dripping with diamonds, brushed seductively against the men, offering a drink, a snippet of conversation, a laugh. A private encounter behind closed doors.

Inside the Panthera, sixteen miles north of Washington, D.C., drinks flowed, deals were made, and powerful men ignored the fact that one of them was a killer.

A woman bumped Grey's arm. "Oh, excuse me."

Her dress, nails, and lips were a matching wine color. Her brown hair was twisted and pinned on top of her head. But those eyes, even with the makeup, screamed young. She couldn't have been legal, and yet according to the Smoking Gun Escort Service, they never hired anyone under twenty.

Yeah, right. And he was the Pope.

The woman grabbed a champagne glass from a passing waitress. "Do you know when the entertainment is supposed to be here?" She turned her big eyes to him over the rim of the glass.

Hazel. Just like Molly's. Grey stuttered. Not now. Don't think of her now. "Entertainment?" Didn't she know she was the entertainment? "You mean the actor running for a senate seat? I believe Chas Loughlin is simply attending tonight's function to talk to the politicians, not to perform."

Hence the increase in security.

"Oh." She gulped the champagne, her gaze now scanning the crowd. "Damn, I was hoping for a distraction."

The vibe she gave off made him curious. Not just young—inexperienced. "First night at the Panthera?"

"How did you...oh, shit," she ducked behind him. "Shit, shit, shit."

He glanced in the direction she'd looked and saw a man who generated a similar response in his own gut. Ahmed Khourey. "The Lion" as Grey had dubbed him, since he prowled the Panthera Leo like he owned the place.

Moving so he blocked the woman from Ahmed's view, he reined in the instant anger boiling inside. "He giving you trouble?"

She waved a hand in the air, signaling a waitress. Another glass of champagne. Another big gulp. "He's handsome and charming and very, very rich." She chuckled. "He's also...intense."

The sound of her soft laugh was so similar to his sister's, Grey flinched. Molly...

Not. Here. "If he's bothering you..."

She downed the last of the champagne, set the empty glass on a nearby bookshelf. Hiked up the fur shawl that had slipped down her shoulders. "I can handle it." Her gaze lifted to his once more. "Thank you."

Before she whisked away, Grey touched her arm and handed her his business card. He resisted telling her she should lay off the booze, that in this place a drunk woman would be easily compromised. "Here's my card if you need... assistance. My personal number is on the back."

She gave him a look that told him she thought he was flirting with her. If she only knew the truth. Sticking the card in her tiny evening bag, she sauntered away, deliberately avoiding The Lion and cozying up to an overweight representative from Alabama.

Grey locked his back teeth and resumed his stance, keeping an eye on her and The Lion.

"What the hell are you doing here?"

The voice came from behind him, but Grey didn't need to turn around to recognize his former boss' irritation. "Since when do they allow FBI agents into the Panthera, Donaldson?"

"The Attorney General invited me."

"Brown-nosing does have its perks I suppose."

Special Agent Harold Donaldson moved so he stood next to Grey. His bland, watery eyes scanned the party as he unbuttoned his too-tight suit jacket. "Since when do they let ex-FBI agents in here?"

Grey held up his ID badge. "Security."

Donaldson snorted as he read the badge. "Jason Black, Front Range Security Specialist. How did you manage that?"

"Front Range has expanded into several new markets, including high-risk security management, bodyguards, and diplomatic protection services. A natural fit for the Panthera."

Another derisive snort. "Let it go, Justice."

So they were using first names now? "Let go of what, Harold?"

The man's bushy eyebrows lowered. "Your obsession with this serial killer is going to land you in jail. Or worse."

Worse had already happened. He'd let women die on his watch. "I don't know what you're talking about. I'm just a lowly security guard making ends meet."

"Ahmed Khourey is not your guy. Look at him." He motioned toward the center of the ballroom where Khourey stood, telling a story about his latest vacation in Africa that involved a run-in with a rhinoceros while hunting big game.

Men and women crowded around him, laughing at his sense of humor and gasping at his narrative of the attack. He was a natural-born storyteller and far more entertaining, Grey bet, than the actor who was due to arrive any minute.

"He doesn't fit a serial killer profile," Donaldson said. "If anything, he's the Lebanese version of the Dos Equis man...the most interesting man in the world."

"Or at least in the Panthera tonight. "Ted Bundy was handsome and charismatic, too."

"You're no longer part of the FBI. Stop obsessing over The Lion. You're chasing the wrong guy."

In his earbud, Grey heard the security supervisor give him the call sign for the actor. "Excuse me, Harold. I have work to do."

FOR MORE WITH GREY, MITCH, AND THE REST OF THE JUSTICE TEAM

Stealing Justice
Cheating Justice
Holiday Justice
Exposing Justice
Undercover Justice
Protecting Justice
Missing Justice
Defending Justice

BOOKS BY ADRIENNE GIORDANO

THE LUCIE RIZZO MYSTERY SERIES
Dog Collar Crime
Knocked Off
Limbo (novella)
Boosted
Whacked
Cooked
Incognito

PRIVATE PROTECTOR SERIES
Risking Trust
Man Law
A Just Deception
Negotiating Point
Relentless Pursuit
Opposing Forces

BOOKS BY MISTY EVANS

SEALS of Shadow Force Series: Spy Division

Man Hunt

Man Killer

Man Down

SEALs of Shadow Force Series

Fatal Truth

Fatal Honor

Fatal Courage

Fatal Love

Fatal Vision

Fatal Thrill

Risk

The SCVC Taskforce Series

Deadly Pursuit

Deadly Deception

Deadly Force

Deadly Intent

Deadly Affair, A SCVC Taskforce novella

Deadly Attraction

Deadly Secrets

Deadly Holiday, A SCVC Taskforce novella

Deadly Target

Deadly Rescue

The Super Agent Series

Operation Sheba

Operation Paris

Operation Proof of Life

The Secret Ingredient Culinary Mystery Series

The Secret Ingredient, A Culinary Romantic Mystery with Bonus Recipes

The Secret Life of Cranberry Sauce, A Secret Ingredient Holiday Novella

---

Sister Witches Of Raven Falls Mystery Series (writing as Nyx Halliwell)

Of Potions and Portents

Of Curses and Charms

Of Stars and Spells

Of Spirits and Superstition

Confessions of a Closet Medium Cozy Mystery Series

(writing as Nyx Halliwell)

(Coming 2020)

CPSIA information can be obtained
at www.ICGtesting.com
Printed in the USA
BVHW060310270220
573386BV00007BB/627